THERE ARE NO DOORS IN DARK PLACES

by

D. G. Valdron

FOSSIL COVE PRESS

Winnipeg, Manitoba

THERE ARE NO DOORS IN DARK PLACES
Fossil Cove Publishing,
1301 - 90 Garry Street,
Wpg, Mb, Can, R3C 4J4

Lanie (short story), previously published by Terminal Fright Magazine (1994) Ed. Kenneth E. Abner, Jr.

Issued in Print and Electronic Format
ISBN: (eBook) 978-1-7771551-2-4,
ISBN: (IngramSpark print/trade paperback) 978-1-998453-22-1

Cover: Photograph and Design by Nancy Arksey, Winnipeg, Manitoba

Text set in Garamond

THERE ARE NO DOORS
IN DARK PLACES

Table of Contents

Introduction

Welcome to my little collection of short stories.

I like horror. People often dismiss it as just being about monsters and such. But the truth is that horror is really about people. People facing monsters, which I admit seems silly...

Unless you are actually facing a monster at the time.

And like it or not, there are monsters in the world. There are plenty of genuine monsters, some quite obvious, rapists, murderers, stalkers, others as subtle as a virus, or pervasive as poverty, as inescapable as cancer. Real monsters are the pleasant date that goes bad, or the clump of cells that goes wild. Or it's just being alone and poor in a cold cruel world, hanging on, without options or prospects.

Real monsters in the world are very hard to face. They're easy to contemplate from a safe distance. But when we actually confront the real things up close and personal; when we come face to face with our own mortality, our own human frailty, that's not easy.

Sometimes with real monsters, there's no way out.

Onwards...

A Long Walk in The Hard Winter

The wind whistled and the snow crunched audibly beneath his feet as he walked. The world felt very empty and desolate, and it seemed to him, that it would be very easy to die out here. Alone and unnoticed.

It was one of those bright midwinter nights, when the moonlight reflected crystalline shimmers on the fresh snow.

He trudged along, cursing his friend Jerry.

His snowmobile was about half a mile behind him. Dead. He wasn't a mechanic. He had no idea how to fix it. He'd have to go pick it up with some friends tomorrow, either get it going in daylight, or have it towed in.

The reason people go snowmobiling in pairs, he thought angrily, was so if one of you got in trouble, the other could stop to help you out.

You weren't supposed to get so far apart that you didn't notice.

He cursed Jerry again.

Still, town was only a few miles away. With luck, Jerry would notice that he was missing and come and pick him up.

He walked. The only sound was the steady crunch of his footsteps on the snowmobile path.

It wasn't a bad winter's night. Brutal cold spells in the early months had given way to a succession of heavy snowfalls. It made for great snowmobiling weather.

Hell on deer though. The cold spells had put pressure on them, and now the snowfalls made it almost impossible for them to move around on their dainty pointed hooves. Some farmers had even taken to leaving bales of hay out, to help them through the winter. You knew it was harsh for animals when farmers started feeding deer.

It made for easy hunting though. You could just drive right up to them. Easy hunting, but poor meat.

Not that there seemed to be any deer left. They were hard to find now, even for poachers.

It occurred to him, as he walked along, his breath hanging visible in the frigid air and the snow crunching under his feet, that he could die out here. It could happen. Just wander off the track for a few yards, he'd be lost. You could freeze to death before they found him. The next snow would cover the body, they might not find him until the spring melt.

He had no illusions about how easy it was to get lost in the woods, or how difficult it was to find someone in time to save them.

He made sure he kept to the path. As long as he was on that, he'd be safe.

The snowmobile path through the woods followed the power transmission line clearance, dipping in and out of meadows and farmers' fields. The power company workers kept trees and bushes from growing along the pathway of the line, making it, in winters, a perfect snow trail. It led straight to town of course; that made it hard to get lost.

He wasn't worried then, just inconvenienced. He cursed Jerry. It helped to pass the time.

Then he noticed the footprint, right beside the particular snowmobile track he was walking on.

He stopped and stared at it.

It was a roughly oblong footprint, with a clearly defined heel, ball and five toes. It was easily twice the length of his own heavy winter boot. It had sunk at least three or four inches into the snow.

A weird thrill ran through him. Some kids in the seventies claimed to have seen one. Crazy Old McPherson claimed to find footprints around his farm from time to time. But then again, Crazy also claimed to see flying saucers.

Briefly, he considered other explanations. A couple of bear prints together? Bears front and hind feet were shaped different, and sometimes a bear's gait would leave one paw print overlapping another, until they looked like a human footprint.

No, You could see from the way the toes gouged the top of the snow as the foot lifted that it wasn't a bear. Besides, there were no claw marks.

A joke then? Some hoax? Could be. But the print looked very authentic.

He looked back the way he came. Now that he was looking for it, he could see a series of depressions in the snow, some in the snowmobile tracks that lead to this print.

It was obviously going in his direction. He turned towards town again, searching.

Yes, there was its mate, a few feet ahead, a left foot print. Not nearly as good though, it was half on, half off a snowmobile track, and had slid, making an indistinct cavity.

Fascinated, he began to follow them, measuring their distance against his best stride. Easily, they were at least twice his.

The footprints generally followed, often laid over, the snowmobile tracks. He supposed that meant they could have been made by jokers on a snowmobile. That would explain the length of the stride. But he didn't think so. Some of the prints were deep; it would take a lot of weight to make them.

Abruptly, he realized that the prints had to be fresh. Some were on top of tracks, none, as far as he could see had been obliterated. They must have been made within the day, maybe even within hours.

He wondered if Jerry had seen them. But there was no place to indicate that a snowmobile had stopped. There were no boot prints around any of the tracks.

As he climbed a rise, a low hill, he realized that Jerry probably wouldn't have spotted them. When you're doing twenty or thirty klicks on a snowmobile at night, you aren't looking for footprints. Especially not ones like these, right beside the trail...

He reached the top of the rise and stopped dead, staring down open mouthed.

It looked up at him, red eyes flashing, and growled.

For a few moments, he was conscious of nothing except his heart thudding inside his chest. His mouth had gone completely dry, and his chest contracted, he couldn't seem to take a breath.

It was crouched in the center of the path, not two dozen feet below him.

Eating.

He was instantly aware of blood drenched snow, steaming pieces of flesh dripping moist, the wreck of a snowmobile a few feet away from it. Don't look at the pieces, he thought, don't look at them, don't recognize them, don't think about it.

They don't bother people, he told himself in astonishment.

Hard goddamned winter, the thought crept through his mind, as if in answer.

As he stared at the half human face, at the powerful, fur covered body, he was vaguely proud that he never even tried to identify it as a bear.

Turn around; just walk back the way you came, was his first coherent thought.

And then where? What next? That way led away from town. It was a good fifteen kilometers before the trail crossed the road and another five before he'd come to a farmhouse.

He'd freeze to death.

Unless it decided to come after him. He'd have to run.

If he ran, it would chase him. It was a natural instinct in all living things. Something runs from you, you chase it. It caught a snowmobile on a dead run, he thought suddenly. If it comes after me, I'm not going to get away.

He stood there, watching it. It stared back angrily. Abruptly it stood up; with quick hands it shoved torn bits of meat, pieces of Jerry, into its mouth until its cheeks bulged.

It barked angrily, spitting little pieces of red gore, black in the moonlight.

It's afraid; he thought suddenly, his heart pounding at the thought. From up here, I'm taller than it is.

Animals attack out of fear as well as anger.

What do I do?

It was growling constantly now, staring at him menacingly. It had stood up, rearing to its full height. It shifted edgily from foot to foot, massive fists balling. He could see heavy muscles hunching in its shoulders.

If I retreat, it'll follow. If I just stand here, it'll eventually work its way up to attacking.

He took a step forward. It watched him, motionless, its eyes narrowing redly. He saw that they reflected light back, like a cat's eyes.

After a long moment, he took another step.

It made a low rumbling noise, deep in its throat.

He took another step. Each footstep took a nightmarish effort of will. It was almost like walking through mud.

I can't go back now, he thought desperately.

Another step.

Again, the low rumbling in the creature's throat. Its shoulders bobbed from side to side. Suddenly it clutched one of the large fragments of the corpse to it defensively.

Another step.

It roared and charged.

Suddenly all he could hear was the pounding of its feet, its angry snarl. It was almost on top of him. He could see its face clearly; its red eyes, the inside of its mouth.

He screamed.

It stopped abruptly, backpedaling several feet.

It growled.

He was drenched in sweat suddenly. He could feel it trickling down the small of his back. His intestines were wound so tight he knew he couldn't vomit, no matter how much he wanted to.

What now? He thought.

An abortive charge. A lethal game of chicken, as it psyched itself up to a killing frenzy.

The creature backed off slowly, never taking its eyes off him. It growled constantly, punctuating it with an occasional angry bark, as it worked its way back to the remains.

It's protecting its kill, he realized.

Now what?

Go around the kill site, flounder off the hard packed snowmobile trails, into the deep snow. He'd poached deer that way, riding up to them as they struggled to take a step.

Abruptly he recalled that sharks attacked humans because their awkward swimming motions seemed like wounded seals.

Wounded, awkward animals were prey.

He visualized himself struggling awkwardly through the deep snow, lifting his legs high, flopping forward, as its long legs and flat feet carried it swiftly, lethally towards him.

He'd made a terrible mistake, he realized, his heart pounding.

It would defend its kill.

He could have gone back. He was suddenly certain of that. He could have stopped at the rise and turned around.

Perhaps before it even saw him. He could have walked slowly away, and it would have stayed with the kill.

What about now?

It was too late, he thought suddenly. I've come too close, I can't retreat.

I can't go forward either.

What would happen if he just kept standing there? He visualized the beast, sitting and snarling as it wolfed down the corpse, spitting as it retreated. Or maybe it would work itself up to attack, enraged by his presence.

With mounting terror, it struck him that all options were equally bad, equally fatal.

Go back then, he decided. Back up slowly; never take your eyes off of it.

Through his mind, vivid images flashed of him backing up, taking a misstep, tripping. The monster on top of him, those slavering fangs about to dig into his face...

NO! With a physical effort he halted his imagination.

One step back.

He couldn't move. He was aware that he was trembling slightly.

One step back. That was all, one little step.

The creature stood. Rapidly, it started gathering all the body parts to itself, holding them in its arms. All of a sudden, it was almost comical as, the more pieces it tried to hold, the more spilled from its arms. Finally, it got them all, holding a large segment in its mouth.

With long strides it stepped off the path, heading for the tree line, never taking its eyes off him. It stopped there and hunkered down, the body part spilling from its mouth as it growled warningly.

It's giving the ground, he realized.

I can pass.

All he had to do was get past it, then it was just a couple of miles to town. Something very much like relief insinuated itself into his guts like a warm liquid serpent.

All he had to do was take a step.

After what seemed like an infinitely long time, he took one.

And then another.

With painfully slow paces he walked up to the place it had been.

It growled softly the whole time.

Their eyes were locked, but through peripheral vision, he could just make out the twisted wreckage of the snowmobile. Black stained half melted snow. Bits of gore.

He saw Jerry's hand in the snow, palm up. It seemed so natural, like Jerry was playing a joke, buried just under, only his palm showing. Ready to give the finger. He tried not to pay attention to it.

As he passed the creature, he had to twist his head further and further to meet its angry red gaze, until finally, he could do it no longer.

He looked away from it, staring down the path between the trees.

He could hear it growling softly behind him.

But that was all it was doing. There was no sound of footsteps after him. No sound of a sudden lethal charge.

Keep going then.

Suddenly, the awful paralysis that had made it so difficult to move had vanished. His muscles leaped.

Don't! He warned himself. Don't run. If he ran, it would chase. If it chased, it would catch. If it caught, he would die. Die horribly.

Carefully, he measured his pace. Walking with careful meticulous steps, he left the monster behind him. Long after he could no longer here it growling, he imagined he could hear it devouring its kill. Devouring his friend.

Tears trickled down his cheeks.

Minutes passed before he found the courage to wipe them.

He walked, setting a careful measured pace. He never looked back. He didn't dare.

He listened intently; his every footfall was like an echo. His senses seemed so taut, he thought he could hear the snow falling; hear the air moving through the trees.

Nothing.

Gradually, an overwhelming familiarity stole over the landmarks. Each tree, each stone and bush, each curve and rise in the trail felt like an old friend, he almost felt that he could have named each of them, if they'd had names.

There was nothing behind him.

All he had to do was turn around and look.

He didn't. He couldn't.

Finally, he topped a hill and looked down at the net of brilliant pinpoints of house lights and street lights of the town below. Warm relief surged through him like a wet current. He fell to his knees and wept, shaking as he finally allowed himself to experience the horror he'd rigidly denied.

Behind him, he heard the heavy dry crunch of a footstep.

The End

Changing Faces

I watched my left forearm ripple and harden, the light brown hairs and pink skin vanishing beneath blunt gray scales. Embarrassed I pulled my sleeve down to conceal it. The jagged surfaces caught on the fabric of my shirt. A ring of scales spread across the back of my hand.

"What's the matter?" Doctor Levin asked.

"It's happening," I told him, and took my hand away.

He stood up from his chair on the other side of the desk to stare closely at my hand. After a moment, he seemed to make a decision and sat down again.

Underneath my clothes I could feel stiff scales poking through the skin as my body struggled to change into something else, something inhuman.

"I'm turning into a monster," I said desperately.

He took off his glasses. After a casual inspection, he began to clean them.

"Help me," I pleaded.

"Tell me how it started," he asked.

A warm flush of fear ran through me. My shoes were becoming unwearable as the bones of my feet changed. I willed it to stop, but I felt it all through me, a sick warm glow that made my stomach knot and my chest ache, like there wasn't enough air for my lungs.

I remembered seeing the Hideous Sun Demon as a kid. It was this movie about a guy who was exposed to radiation; it twisted his chromosomes so that whenever he was out in the sun, he would start devolving into a human iguana.

"Could you get the blinds, please," I requested, "the sun's really bothering me."

Wordlessly he got up and stepped over to the window. He closed the blinds completely and returned to his seat. He waited.

I felt the changing recede slowly from my body.

"It started with the accident," I said.

"No," he said, "I meant tell me about the first time something happened."

He paused.

"The first time you felt something happen," he corrected himself.

Nervously, I ran my tongue around the inside of my mouth, against my teeth. It was too sinuous, and the teeth were too jagged, sliding against each other like a series of razor blades.

"Well," I began, "it was about a month ago, on the seventeenth. Two weeks after the accident. Nancy, my wife, was down with the flu, so I had to get Regan-"

"Regan?" he asked, making a note.

"My daughter," I explained, "our daughter, mine and Nancy's. She's about seven years old."

He nodded, "go on."

I was a little annoyed. I assumed that Nancy would have told him about Regan. Nancy had talked me into coming here, and I supposed she would have told him about our lives. I felt like he was testing me.

"Anyway," I continued, "I had to get Regan off to school myself. After that, I went to the bathroom to brush my teeth and get washed up. That's when I noticed it."

"Yes," he said.

"Teeth," I explained. "When I was brushing my teeth, I saw them there, in the mirror, in a mouthful of toothpaste. Fangs."

"It's hard to describe what it was like. Imagine waking up and discovering you've got an extra nostril, or another hand.

It wasn't just that I saw them; I felt them, with my tongue, with the toothbrush. They were physically present."

He was just watching me.

"I rinsed out my mouth to examine them. They were two fangs, about an inch long. Right here," I bared my teeth and indicated the corners of my mouth, "sharp enough to prick my finger."

"They looked very natural there; they even had a little bit of tartar in the corner. All my other teeth were the same; these had just squeezed in somehow. The lower teeth were unaffected."

"I was looking at them, just sort of puzzled by the whole thing, when I noticed the other part."

"Which was?" the psychologist asked.

"I wasn't breathing. I hadn't taken a breath for a minute and a half. I didn't feel the need to, either."

"You were a vampire," he stated.

I nodded, "I didn't realize it at first, you know. It was all so sudden and out of context that I wasn't putting the pieces together. I mean, according to the stories, you have to get bitten, be buried and so forth."

I gestured futilely. "I mean you aren't supposed to turn into a vampire while brushing your teeth just after you've packed your daughter off to school."

He nodded.

"I'd pricked my finger, but it wasn't bleeding. I exhaled and waited three and a half minutes. I held my face really close to the mirror, so I could see the mist, but there wasn't any."

"It wasn't like adding two and two. In this case, four was an unacceptable number. An impossible number. It was so completely irrational; my mind wouldn't willingly accept it. Instead, over fifteen minutes, I just became gradually aware of it, to the point where I could think 'vampire.'"

I looked at him.

"I know how hard it must be for you to accept. It was happening to me, and I wasn't accepting it."

"How did you feel?" he asked, "Any urge to drink blood?"

"I felt...weirded out," I said, remembering, "my wife was in the bedroom, sleeping. Suddenly, there was this thing inside, a hunger, and I knew it wanted me to go in there and tear her throat out. It wanted to drink her blood."

He was making notes again.

"It wasn't me. And there was no doubt in my mind that I wasn't going to do it. It wasn't very strong. It was like a far, far away, voice. It was just..." I struggled, "a component of the change."

"Then what happened?" he asked.

"I couldn't believe it, I had to test this. I went downstairs and walked out into the morning sun."

"That was when your wife heard you screaming," he said.

"And half the neighbors," I finished for him, "I wound up with horrible sunburns. They lasted for a week. She saw them."

He nodded. So, she had told him about that, I thought.

"But you were back to normal?" he asked.

It was my turn to nod.

"What did you make of that episode?"

"I certainly didn't tell Nancy. What could I say: 'honey, I turned into a vampire this morning while brushing my teeth, but I feel much better now.' I thought maybe it was some sort of weird hallucination."

"Have you ever had hallucinations?" he asked.

"No. Never," I answered emphatically.

"Ever taken psychedelic drugs? Mushrooms? LSD? Things like that?"

"No."

"What about your mother?"

"What?" I asked, confused.

"LSD stores in body fat. It's rare but sometimes it's passed through the placental membrane into infants, and can kick in after the birth."

"I don't think so," I said dubiously.

He made more notes.

"It wasn't a hallucination," I said firmly.

"You believe that now," he said, emphasizing the last word.

"I do," I said with equal emphasis.

"What changed your mind?" he asked.

"It happened again, a couple of nights later."

"You turned into a vampire again?"

"Worse," I told him, "I was lying in bed, next to Nancy, dozing. I felt this tingling all over my body. I looked down..."

He waited expectantly.

"I was growing fur all over. Suddenly, I could feel my body changing, pulling into a new shape, my teeth flowing. My teeth, Doctor, turning into fangs. Not just one or two, but the whole mouthful."

"That far away voice I mentioned? It was back. It was like a wild beast now. Full of power and destruction. It wanted me to tear things apart, to seize flesh and bite and rend it."

"What happened?"

"I just lay there, for an hour, not believing it, fighting it."

"Then Nancy rolled over in her sleep. She touched me. She felt it, Doctor, she felt the fur. She started to wake up. That was when I knew I had to do something. I leaped from the bed, and raced for the bathroom."

"Where she found you shaving off all your body hair," he said.

"Fur, Doctor," I told him, "I had to shave the fur off. The bathroom was covered with it; she saw it, when she came in."

"She said that you were mumbling incoherently, in a state of panic."

"I couldn't open my mouth in front of her, the teeth hadn't changed back," I explained, "and I was in a state of panic. Wouldn't you be?"

"So you'd changed into a werewolf?"

"Look," I said, reaching into my wallet, "here's proof. I saved this from that night."

I pulled out a lock of hair and dropped it on his desk.

"That's from me," I told him, "genuine werewolf fur. I filled a small garbage bag with that stuff."

He looked at it, bending over the desk, holding his glasses. But he didn't touch it.

"It's happened again and again, since then," I told him, "sometimes I start turning into some sort of ape. Once in the bathtub, I developed gill slits. Once my skin went all translucent. Another time, I started to glow and I killed everything that was near me. I can show you the dead patch in the garden."

"I'm interested in these atavistic feelings you have when you change," he stated.

"It's like a radio playing low in the next room," I told him, it's distant and uninvolving. You know it's there, but you don't pay attention to it, aren't affected by it. It's just a part that comes from the changes."

My voice was coming rapidly, cracking, I reined in my panic.

"I keep turning into monsters, Doctor. I'm afraid and I feel so alone."

"You watched a lot of horror movies as a child?"

"Of course," I responded, "so did everyone else."

"Your wife tells me," he said gravely, "that when you were a boy, you thought your father was a monster."

The change of topics threw me.

"Yeah, so," I answered.

He waited.

"There wasn't anything to that: Late at night, he'd check to see if I was all right. The door would open, and he'd stand there, a dark silhouette against the hall light. I used to imagine that he looked like different monsters. Frankenstein one night, the wolfman another."

"No big deal," I went on, "kids imagine stuff like that all the time. My best friend back then, Jimmy Deacon, had this really scary tree overlooking his bedroom window. In the dark, on winter nights, it looked like it was trying to get in."

"But you thought your father was a monster," he said, "a wolfman."

"There's nothing there, it was just a kid's imagination," I told him defensively. I was sweating suddenly.

"What happened after he appeared in the doorway?" he asked.

"Nothing. I went to sleep," I said. I looked around the room, avoiding eye contact with the Doctor.

"What time would he come?" he asked.

"I don't know," I answered, irritably, "bedtime I suppose."

Why was he on this tangent? I wished he'd stop.

I could feel the scales starting to squirm. We stared at each other for a second.

"Tell me what you think it is," he asked.

"I had an accident," I said. I spoke challengingly.

He didn't say anything.

"It was a bad one. The car was totaled; I'd collided with a truck."

"You had a severe concussion," he offered, "you were unconscious for several hours. That can cause strange behavior."

"People have accidents all the time. Even bad ones," I said, "they don't start turning into monsters. This truck was carrying something."

"Go on."

"Agricultural pharmaceuticals," I told him, "I managed to check up on some of them later. Do you know what Anaphasin is?"

"What?" he asked.

"It's a brand name for thalidomide. The truck was full of it...and other things."

I let him digest this.

"I didn't believe thalidomide was allowed in this country."

"Not for humans," I said, "it turns out it's pretty common as an animal tranquilizer."

He looked at me.

"Don't you see," I explained, "it's derailed my genetic structure. My chromosomes are mutating because of my exposure to the truck."

"Into vampires and werewolves," he scoffed.

"It's happening," I insisted, "I know it sounds crazy, but this is really happening and that's the only explanation I can find. Maybe it's something else that's causing it, a quantum mechanic effect or something; but this is real."

"I'm a psychologist," he said.

"I know that," I said.

"You aren't a geneticist, or a chemist, or a biologist," he went on.

Once again, we had one of those short moments of standoff.

"You have the fur," I told him, "that's real. The dead patch in the garden is real. Nancy's seen parts of the changes, like the sunburn. I can show you footprints and claw marks all over the house. You've seen my hand..."

I stood up and tore open my shirt, exposing the last cluster of grey scales, before they faded, "I can show you this," I snarled at him.

He stared for a second and then pulled his eyes away.

"All I see is normal human flesh," he said softly, "all I saw was a normal hand."

I slumped back in the chair.

"Of course," I said, "that's all you can see, all you'll allow yourself to see."

"Explain," he requested.

"I saw a collection of Japanese historical prints once, it was from the time of the Great White Fleet, when the Americans sailed into Japan and forced the country to open up. It was funny: All the drawings of the Americans, their clothing and their ships, made them look Japanese."

"Americans were outside their existence, in order to deal with them, they had to think of them as looking Japanese. They could only see them from their own frame of reference."

"Don't you see?" I asked, "Grey scales on a human being are outside your frame of reference, you see it and then your mind rejects it, and instead you see something that your mind will accept."

"Doesn't say much for the human mind," he said, "it's a wonder that we can deal with novelty."

"If I suddenly became dangerous; a grey skinned lizardman- with fangs and talons, then you'd see. Self-preservation would force you."

"Is that a threat?" he asked quietly.

"No," I sighed, "it's just the way our minds work. You can't accept this, and if I wasn't inside it, I wouldn't either.

"Let me suggest this alternative hypothesis:" he said, "You are hallucinating, the shape of these hallucinations may be related to your past, but the fact that you are having them relates to the severe concussion you suffered in the accident."

"I'm not insane, Doctor," I told him coldly.

"I didn't say you were," he said, "it's not a term we like to use."

"I'm not hallucinating. I'm trying to deal with this rationally. I am rational," I told him.

"Yes," he agreed, "you are rational. But rational people can have delusions."

I stood up, "good day, Doctor."

"I think we should discuss this again," he began.

"I don't think so," I told him coldly.

"One thing," he called.

I turned back at the doorway.

"Vampires can't be seen in mirrors," he said.

"The change wasn't finished at that point," I replied.

As I left the office, I found Nancy waiting for me. I hugged her. Under my clothes, I could feel the scales twisting in my flesh, fading again.

"Did it help?" she asked me.

"No," I answered.

We wrapped our arms around each other, clinging miserably.

On the way back, as Nancy drove, I discovered that my right hand had become a chitinous claw, glossy black, covered with stiff wire-like hairs, and ending in a series of sharp delicate pincers. I stuck it into my jacket pocket, and turned my face to the passenger window. Sometimes, in the reflection, I caught glimpses of faceted eyes.

At least with cancer, I thought, people understand. They gather around. But this, with this, I had nothing but ever increasing terror. Fear of the future, of myself, of what I might turn into. No one understands this.

Was it triggered by things I did, or things I saw? By foods? Emotions? I wasn't sure. Even when I was completely human, I felt myself withdrawing more and more into myself. Avoiding emotions, avoiding people, hiding from anything that might spur the change.

I felt myself hiding from Regan and Nancy. Not allowing myself to touch either of them. How long had it been since I had dared to make love to Nancy? I missed her touch, missed holding her in the night.

I was all alone with it, and the only response I seemed to have was to become more alone with it. With my fear.

Late one night, they came for me.

Doctor Levin had signed the commitment papers after the interview, at Nancy's request.

They must have expected a struggle. I surprised them by going quietly. I didn't have the heart to fight. Nancy wouldn't look up at me, as they lead me away.

I didn't see her again for two weeks. Two weeks, and endless changes, as my flesh crawled back and forth.

Once, I was a skeleton, lying on the bed as my flesh oozed gelatinously along the floor.

Once, I became a nameless thing of tentacles and eyes and open sucking mouths which writhed hungrily.

Night after night, my body, my fickle friend, betrayed me.

When she came, I'd become the mummy, Kharis. Buried immortal for two thousand years. I sat hunched stiffly in the wheelchair, all but immobile.

She looked awful. I wanted to speak, but my throat could no longer form human words. I wanted to weep, but centuries of Egyptian desert had leached the moisture from my body.

In the back of my mind I could hear the dry voice from the land of the Pharaohs.

"Jerome," she said, "Jerome, can you hear me?"

Painstakingly, I nodded. I moved my free arm forward, until I could clasp her hand. I was careful not to crush it.

Oh darling, I thought, how much I've missed you and Regan. I wished that she'd brought our daughter. But then, I realized, I didn't want my daughter to see me like this.

"They say you aren't responding to conventional treatment," she said.

"The hospital Doctors want me to authorize a new treatment for you," her voice broke, "they say it's safe now. Not like the old days. They say it's the only hope."

Tears rolled down her eyes. I could not cry.

"Electro-convulsive therapy," she said.

No, I screamed inside, not that. Don't kill my mind, I thought, it's all I have. It's my body that's gone wrong. Inside is all I have left.

"They say it's for the best," she said.

"Please," I tried to make an ages old throat speak, "please don't do this to me."

All that passed was a coarse moan.

She looked into my stiff desiccated face, sobbed once, and left.

Please don't kill me inside, I begged. But no words came, and there was no one to hear them.

That afternoon, they came for me again.

It was another month and a half, before I was released from the hospital. It was early evening when Nancy picked me up. We drove home without speaking, I watched the sky get dark.

Regan met us at the door. She'd persuaded the babysitter to let her stay up to greet me. She rushed into my arms.

"I missed you, Daddy," she smiled.

I lifted her up and held her close to me. Her small warm body felt good. I looked into her smiling face, "Daddy, missed you too, Pumpkin."

She had cupids bow lips. Odd that I'd never noticed her promiscuous child sexuality before. She was going to be a heartbreaker, I decided.

I kissed her.

I put her down. We grinned at each other, glad to be together again.

"Are you still turning into monsters?" she asked, she'd always accepted it with equanimity, even glee. After all, having a dad who turned into movie monsters was almost as good as having a dad who was a movie star.

"There are no monsters, dear. It was just a funny idea your Dad had. Those Doctors burned it right out of him. Now he's just me."

I spread my arms to show her: Just Daddy, just human old Daddy. No scales or talons or fur, nothing different on the outside. I looked just like everyone else.

"It's past your bedtime," I told her, "run on upstairs, Daddy'll be up to check on you, and tomorrow, we'll do all kinds of things."

As Nancy paid off the babysitter, I watched Regan's round tight buttocks bounce up the stairs. I definitely would have to pay her a visit tonight, I promised myself. But first, there was Nancy to deal with.

We were alone. She looked nervous.

"Are you feeling all right, Jerome?" she asked, "You seem ... odd."

"Never better," I told her, "I'm cured after all."

"Doctor Levin said he'd like you to continue treatment," she said, "he felt that you had unresolved issues, to do with your father."

I took a step towards her.

"I don't see any need. I've had treatment, I'm fine," I replied.

"Doctor Levin argued against your 'treatment'," she said. "He thought your 'transformations' were a symptom, not the problem itself. He suggested that maybe it was your way of coping with the real problem."

She took a step back.

"Symptoms? Problems? What's the difference? I'm not turning into movie monsters anymore. I feel much...better." I smiled reassuringly, she looked uncertain, almost afraid.

I took another step.

"There's something different about you," she whimpered, "you aren't the Jerome I know."

"I'm your husband," I told her, "look at me."

"Jerome, please..." she said, and then I was on her.

She didn't even have time to scream.

Later, after I finished with Nancy, I went upstairs.

The End

Lanie

The feeder strolled down the street, past men and women, its sensitive tendrils quivering for the warm scent of host. Its manbrain whined a complaint, but the feeder ignored it. It was hungry.

* * *

Lanie shivered in the cold welfare waiting room. It was winter outside and she thought she could see her breath even here. It was an ugly room, cold and sparse with gray walls and too many bodies in it. Protectively, she ran her hand down her distended stomach.

The room was crowded with supplicants. A lot of them were women, young women and old women, sick ones and healthy ones. Some looked like they'd been on welfare their entire lives, they seemed resigned. Others looked embarrassed and ashamed to be there. A handful had taken their children with them, hoping to win an earlier place in line. The cries of squalling infants cut through the air. Welfare hated people who brought their children and tended to deal with them quickly.

Everyone shared a look of hard edged desperation. But then, she thought, nobody who was not desperate would want to spend their afternoon at the Welfare Office.

The security guard finally called out her name. She climbed laboriously to her feet and made her way past reproving and resigned stares. Her worker was waiting for her on the other side of the plate (bulletproof?) glass doors. The security guard regarded her levelly from his booth as she showed him her

Welfare Photo ID and handed him her bag. She noticed that he wore a gun. She stepped through the detector.

It was much warmer on the other side. The Worker stepped up to her radiating false friendliness. She almost seemed like she was going to take Lanie's hand, but she knew she wouldn't. No contact with the clients. It was one of their rules.

"Hello Lanie," the Worker said, "I'm Kathleen. Do you remember me from your last visit?"

Lanie simply nodded. She remembered, but she wasn't sure that the worker did. She figured that the Worker saw hundreds of clients each month and didn't remember any of them. Lanie thought the worker just checked her file for her Client's last contacts before actually meeting them.

The Worker led Lanie to a neat little cubicle. The desk was cluttered with papers and a big plastic sunflower blossom stood in a glass of water by the desk. On the walls of the cubicle were agency posters and bright children's drawings.

The Worker sat; her eyes briefly skimmed her file. She looked up to Lanie.

"You are still living at suite 32, 686 Ash Boulevard?"

Lanie nodded.

"I see Ms Gomez did a home study there two weeks ago," she glanced to the file again, "It went very well."

Lanie shrugged. Her eyes lingered over the Workers immaculately manicured and painted fingernails. Lanie thought that she could probably do work like that, she'd had some training.

"Is anyone living with you there, Lanie?" the Worker asked. They always used your name when they wanted to be serious.

"No."

"You're sure now. Do you have a boyfriend, Lanie?"

"No."

"Maybe he sleeps over every now and then? How often Lanie?"

"I told you, I don't have a boyfriend. I'm alone," Lanie insisted.

The Social Worker looked up from her file. Measuring her.

"Do you drink, Lanie?"

She shook her head.

"What about drugs?"

Again the head shake.

"It isn't just for your own good Lanie. We are concerned about your baby too. You have a responsibility."

Lanie nodded miserably.

"As long as you are on assistance we can make you take tests. For your own good."

"I know," Lanie mumbled. She knew they wouldn't require drug tests unless they suspected something. They were just too expensive to administer randomly.

"You are due in six months," the Worker said, checking her file.

"One month," Lanie corrected.

The worker looked at Lanie's stomach for the first time.

"I see, and this explains your application for pre-natal benefits?"

Lanie assented. The Worker made a show of looking over the application form.

"Why do you think you need these benefits, Lanie?"

"Babies clothes, diapers, toys n' things...food," Lanie mumbled. It was in the form and they both knew it.

"Uh huh," the Worker went. "The application doesn't show any name for the father."

Lanie shrugged.

"Do you know the father, Lanie?"

She shook her head. The Worker grew accusing.

"You must realize that the father of your child has a responsibility too. It shouldn't just be the taxpayers taking care of things. He should contribute."

Lanie just sat there dumb and mute. The Worker drummed her fingers against her desk.

"This can endanger your entitlements. You know that."

"No it can't," Lanie answered.

At least not until they changed the welfare rules, and that wouldn't be for another couple of years at least.

They stared at each other.

Finally the Worker straightened up in her chair. She picked up a pen and signed the application. She handed it to Lanie.

"Take this to the Auditor's booth. They'll issue you a check. After that it will just go on to your biweekly entitlement until the baby is born and we'll change it to a post-natal entitlement."

Lanie pushed herself to her feet, holding the paper in one hand she went off to collect her bag. Behind her the Worker made her notes for the file.

"Uncooperative," she wrote.

* * *

It was afternoon when she finally left the Welfare Offices, and a cold wind was blowing down the street. But Lanie felt almost elated. She was out of there, and she had money. Not a lot of money, she understood that. Nor would it last long, she understood that too. But at least it was money.

Now she had to decide how to spend it. Many of the things she would need, like diapers and pads were expensive at the small local stores in her neighborhood. It would be better to go to one of the big places like Safeway, but it was a long way off. The bus wouldn't let her ride if she had too many parcels, and it would be too far to walk with any kind of load. She might make several bus trips, but that would cost money and she didn't have that many bus vouchers left.

On the spur of the moment, she decided to treat herself. She stopped in at a corner restaurant and sat on one of the stools. The menu hung in plastic letters in a board above the counter. She studied it, balancing her hunger against what she could afford.

The waitress came by. She ordered a BLT with a slice of Pie. Blueberry was on special. And a cup of tea, please. The waitress jotted down the order and moved on.

While she waited Lanie noticed a sign in the corner. 'Dishwasher Wanted.' She could do that, she thought.

She imagined herself working as a dishwasher. Working with other people. Getting a paycheck. Not having to go to the Welfare Office again.

She sipped her tea and let the fantasy grow. Maybe she could even learn enough to become a cook. Better yet a waitress. She imagined meeting new people every day, serving them food, getting paid, and tips on top. She could eat leftovers at the restaurant, not have to spend so much money on food.

"Looks like we got the same stomach, you and me."

Lanie turned to the voice that had interrupted her reverie. Not much of a fantasy anyway, she thought, who was going to hire a seven or eight month pregnant teenager? Afterward, how would she be able to maintain a job when she had to look after an infant twenty-four hours a day?

The man who had spoken was older. In his twenties or thirties. He hadn't shaved in a day or two, and hadn't bathed in longer. His hair was a little stringy and thinner than it had once been, and his teeth didn't look so good. But, he had an engaging smile and friendly eyes. The pot belly he had referred to protruded from his jacket and over the top of his jeans.

"In a month or two I'll be thin," she told him haltingly, "How about you?"

He laughed easily, reassuring her.

"Not that quick," he replied, "But that reminds me of a story I heard..."

He told it well and she found herself laughing. It wasn't a big laugh or anything. But it was funny and friendly and she hadn't heard the story before.

Encouraged, he told another. She liked that one too. Soon they were talking. He was new in town. Looking for work, just him and his 1998 Ford Toronado, his girlfriend had tossed him out.

She'd lived here all her life. It was an alright place she thought. She didn't say if she had a boyfriend or not, but he didn't ask.

What was she going to call the baby? Max for a boy, Maxine for a girl. That was a good name, he allowed. She told him she had gotten the idea from a nighttime soap opera on one of the two channels she could get off the airwaves.

He told her he knew a way to steal cable channels. He was used to doing all sorts of things to make his way. His name was Jeff, by the way. She said she was called Lanie, after an old movie star. He thought that was a good name too. She said it was all right.

She told him her favorite movie was Pretty Woman. He knew it too. He said it was his too, but mainly, he admitted, for the dirty parts. She laughed, charmed by his shy grin. He ordered ice cream, and as an afterthought ordered some for her too.

It was good to talk to someone. It felt good, simply to talk to someone new. Lanie found herself slipping into new topics, just to prolong this little pleasure, until finally she noticed the time.

"I'm late," she said, feeling oddly like the princess in the fairy tale, "I have to get my stuff before the stores close."

She winced to see disappointment flicker across his face.

"I could drive you around," he offered, "I got a car. It's just about all I got right now."

She half smiled at his small joke.

"No, I don't want to put you to the trouble."

He shrugged.

"It's no trouble. I don't have anything else to do now anyway," he seemed honest and sincere. It was as if she was the first nice person he had met since coming here and he didn't want to lose touch.

Still, Lanie decided, she wasn't going to go walking down some back alley with him no matter how nice he seemed.

"Where's your car?" she asked.

He jerked his finger out the window.

"Just across the street. It's the blue and rust one."

"Okay," she said.

As they were going out one of the local street people started shambling toward her. It was a big hairy old man with a face like leather and rheumy eyes. Lanie hated them. A few weeks ago one evening, one of them, a bearded old man had followed her for four blocks. Finally she had broken and run the last block home. She could hear him wheezing all the way behind her.

Jeff stepped easily, unconsciously, between them. She breathed a sigh of relief. Lanie crossed the street with him. Behind her she could hear the beggar wheeze. It reminded her of the other one.

Jeff opened the passenger door for her and waited for her to get in, closing it behind her, just like a chauffeur.

He got in the driver's side, turned the starter, it whined. He pumped the gas and hit the starter again. Finally it turned over.

"So what do you think?" he asked, grinning. She could see that he was proud of his car. "It doesn't look like much, but it runs good."

There Are No Doors in Dark Places – Page 33

She looked around. The dashboard was cracked and the seats were covered with blankets, but she could tell that the vinyl had split and foam rubber had spilled out. There was a faint smell of machine oil. But the car was reasonably clean and she could feel the motor purring smoothly.

"It's okay," she said "It sounds good, doesn't knock or anything."

"Thanks," he seemed boyishly happy, "I changed the motor myself, just before I left."

He pulled out into traffic.

The bearded beggar was staring at Lanie, his eyes boring into her from across the street. She imagined that she could hear his wheezing, identical to the wheezing she had heard the other night.

Jeff drove on, unconcerned.

* * *

The feeder smelled a host, had come close enough to taste the chemical soup radiated by a gravid human woman. Deep within, tendrils coiled in anticipation of capturing and devouring. It scourged the manbrain. But the manbrain only cringed and advocated caution. The feeder waited.

* * *

They went to the SuperValu that was all the way across town, because she'd seen several bargains in a flyer.

Lanie had a great time shopping. It was mostly drab and utilitarian commodities that went into her shopping cart. All best buys and no name brands. But it was fun just to be able to go on a major shopping expedition and it was fun to be in a different store. Boredom was the major component of her life in poverty. The same people, the same stores, the same offices, the same lonely four walls. With Jeff around people simply seemed nicer. She was amused when one service person treated them obviously as a couple.

"Why'd your girlfriend throw you out?" Lanie asked him as they were looking at baby formula.

"Lost my job," he seemed embarrassed by the question, he looked vulnerable suddenly, "There was more, I guess. But that's what it all came down to. Mainly my fault."

She felt a wave of sympathy for him.

"Don't be hard on yourself. People are always blaming themselves for things that happen. But a lot of the time they didn't get into a mess by themselves," Lanie indicated her swollen stomach. "Look at me."

They didn't talk about it again.

Jeff bought a few things for her. But when Lanie realized how little money he had she made him stop. He just shrugged and grinned.

She saved some money on the trip. Not a lot, but some, and every bit counted. Cheered, Lanie and Jeff chatted enthusiastically on the way back.

It was getting dark. More and more of the street people were coming out. She watched them from the safety of the car. Did some of them turn to watch her go by? Lanie decided she was just being paranoid, and forced herself to concentrate on the conversation with Jeff.

The trip across town to her place went quickly. They laughed as Jeff parked beside Lanie's building, a rundown brownstone, and they loaded up with plastic bags and boxes.

Lanie felt a shiver of embarrassment as she opened the door to her two room apartment.

"This is my place," she told him, almost reluctant to flick the light switch to display the ratty collection of second hand furniture that decorated her home.

The door opened onto the room she slept in, with a couple of queen sized mattresses in a corner served as a bed, and a couple of tousled sheets and blankets covering them. The first room opened into the second, a rickety coffee table

with an old TV set divided them. One of the coffee tables
legs was so loose; she had actually had to stuff its juncture
with cardboard wedges to stabilize it. A corner of the second
room had been converted to a kitchenette; beside it was the
doorway to the bathroom. The furniture was sparse and old.

Jeff didn't say much as he helped her put away the things.

Finally they finished. Jeff stuck his hands in his pockets.

"Well, I guess this is it."

"Uh, yeah," Lanie said.

"It was nice talking to you."

Lanie wanted him to stay. She didn't want to return to
four lonely walls, hiding away from street people.

"Same here," she said, shifting from one foot to another.

"See you around," he said, and then he was gone.

Lanie watched the door shut behind him. It was a flimsy
door, she thought, with a bad lock. It was suddenly colder in
the room.

She sat down on the bed for a moment. She leaned
forward and turned on the television. A black and white
image swelled and rolled.

Restless, Lanie got up from the bed and went to the
window in the other room, watching for Jeff.

He didn't appear. She could see his car from her window.
Seconds turned into minutes. Still, he didn't appear.
Gradually she became aware of a derelict squatting in
shadows across the street.

Involuntarily she pulled into the edge of her window. Was
he staring at her window? At her? She could just make out
that it was male, and bearded. The wheeze that had pursued
her came back into her mind.

Lanie headed back to her bedroom to turn the lights off.
Perhaps he wouldn't stare at a dark window. He could stare at
something else. Maybe she could see better without a light
behind her.

There Are No Doors in Dark Places – Page 36

Lanie wondered what happened to Jeff. In the dark a twisted little fantasy of cannibal street people flitted through her mind.

She heard heavy steps coming up the stairs. Her heart started to pound. Lanie chided herself for her fear. It was just, she thought, that she didn't know anyone in this building. Wasn't used to the place. It was dark out.

The footsteps came down the hall, approaching her door. She sat on the bed, half watching the TV, half watching the door. She slid her fingers under her pillow to the steak knife she kept there.

Lanie watched the doorknob turn. Her heart caught in her throat as she realized that it hadn't locked when Jeff left. That she hadn't heard the familiar click of the door shutting completely. For a moment it was like a weight on her chest, she couldn't breathe, she clutched the knife. The door swung open.

"Why'd you turn off the light?" Jeff asked, standing in the doorway, blinking. In his left hand he clutched a roll of tape and a couple of long wires.

Suddenly she could breathe again. She released the knife under her pillow.

"Uh...I was going to watch TV."

He grinned, flicking on the light.

"That's great. I found the cable box for the building. I think I rigged a patch for you, so that you can get all the channels."

He held up the cable wire.

"That's really nice. Thanks," she said elated. He had come back.

"No problem," he was looking for the wall jack. Finding it, he knelt with the tape and wire. Lanie made sure the door was locked this time.

"Listen, why don't you turn to an empty channel and we'll see if this works," Jeff prompted her.

"Okay," she said. She sat on the bed and turned the little black and white to static. She watched him work.

He got up and began to fix the wire to the television set. Abruptly the static vanished and Jeopardy appeared. Lanie gave a little giggle of pleasure.

Jeff sat down on the bed next to her. He reached out and flicked from one channel to another.

"It's too bad it's such an old TV. You're only going to get the channels that are on the dial."

"That's all right," she reassured him, "It's a lot better than what I had before."

Lanie put her hand on his arm.

"Thanks," she said.

They were both still for a moment, sitting together on the bed. Lanie felt a need, an urge to do something more.

"So," she said, "are you hungry? I could make you something to eat?"

He looked at her.

"That would be nice," he said gravely. He bent towards her.

"I know you're new in town. If you don't have any place to stay," she found herself going on, "you could stay here for a while, just until you found a place."

She found herself bending towards him. "It would be better than sleeping in your car." she whispered.

They kissed. It was a small kiss at first, tentative in its contact. It ebbed and flowed like a tide, their lips moving against each other.

Lanie felt his arms rise up uncertainly to embrace her, to hold her. She accepted them, reached out to touch him herself. Her fingertips slid along his forearm. Their heads and necks swayed slowly together as they kissed. The kiss slowly but easily passing through stages of intensity.

Lanie felt his hand gently caress the tender swell of her breast. With slow circular movements he teased her nipples to erection. His hands on her were soft and knowing. Her lips parted and his tongue slid into her mouth, exploring her with disturbing intelligence.

She concentrated on his hands. She let him unbutton her blouse. Reveled in his touch of her bare skin, he slipped under her bra to cup her bare swollen breast in his hand. His other hand caressed her distended stomach.

She let him lay her down on the bed. She luxuriated in his tenderness. It felt good to be touched, to be held. It was good to be loved. It had been a long time.

She felt him fumbling with the clasp of her jeans, and then heard her zipper fall. He began to work them down her thighs.

"Not this close to the baby," Lanie whispered to him, "I can do other things for you. But not that."

He grunted softly, and his body pressed against hers. But he continued to pull her jeans down. She pushed against him, whispering to do other things. He pushed back. She felt his hardness, almost throbbing in his pants.

A streak of ice sliced through Lanie's romantic glow. For a moment she was uncertain. She wiggled and struggled. He matched her, always exerting just a little more force than she did. What if she tried hard, made it a clear no, and he did it anyway? Better to have some control and go along, rather than to push so hard that she might find he gave her no choice whatsoever. She didn't want to face that.

The ice grew in her. Part of it was concern for the baby.

Part of it was revulsion at the perversion that would hunger for a pregnant woman. It was as if he wasn't interested in her, but in her pregnancy.

"Jeff, No." There. She had said it clearly.

He didn't stop. Lanie began to struggle. He lay on top of her, holding her down with sheer weight. Her jeans were off. She could feel his knee, knifing between her thighs, spreading them. Her arms were pinned. She tried to scream. He covered her mouth with one hand. For a moment one arm was free.

She clawed at his face, two fingers traced the curve of one orbit. She drove them into the eye, feeling a stomach turning jelly coolness.

Jeff screamed, his back arching, blood running down his face. She slipped from under him and he fell on the bed, across the pillows. Escape filled Lanie's mind, she slid out onto the floor beside the TV, trying to crawl away. Her ankles were tangled in her jeans. She had hurt him badly, she was afraid he was going to try and hurt her even worse, terror clouded her mind.

She felt his fingers digging into her back, twisting in her hair, and she screamed again. The back of her blouse ripped, the fabric biting into her shoulders. He pulled her off the floor by her scalp. Her hands scrabbled out for any purchase. Lanie's fingers touched the leg of the coffee table, seized them. The table leg came loose in her hand. Unbalanced the table tilted, the little black and white television tipped over, its picture tube exploding as it smashed into the floor. Lanie screamed and swung at her attacker.

The first blow glanced off his arm. She swung again, catching him in the face with the table leg. More blood was flowing. She was obscenely aware of his erection thrusting from his trousers. She swung again with all her strength, felt bone give, he staggered. Grunting he reached for the club. She swung again, but he caught it, and wrenched it from her grip.

Suddenly, she was flying through the air. She hit the wall on the other side of the bed, and fell. She felt her baby kick, inside her. Her nose was bleeding.

Lanie saw him standing there, swaying. His face was covered with blood, his head was split open. His erection had forced itself farther out of his trousers; it was monstrous, a foot and a half, even two feet long. It twisted and writhed with a will of its own, flinging itself from side to side as the body swayed, as if seeking her. Lanie's stomach turned. She began to scream again.

* * *

The feeder was enraged. It had allowed the manbrain to stalk the host. Come so close that it could taste the composition of the unknown fetus. It had been ready to invade the womb of the host and devour the unborn. Now it was all snatched away. The manbrain screamed its pain down the linkages of their shared nervous system; left to itself, the manbrain would have simply collapsed.

The feeder rammed surges of agony up to the manbrain, forcing it into submission. It responded clumsily. The feeder extended its control through their nervous and circulatory systems, forcing the muscles to co-operate with the limp guidance of the manbrain.

It smelled host.

* * *

Lanie scrabbled for the door, screaming. But it wouldn't open. Locked. She felt the shape behind her. Struggled as it picked her up and flung her onto the bed.

"Itilll beee goood," it slurred. Up close it was nightmarish, one eye was gone leaving only a bleeding socket, the skin along the side of the forehead had split open, leaving hanging rags of flesh, the bone was exposed and cracked.

"Yuulllle Seeee," it crooned. It was on top of her. Fumbling at her. It seemed less co-ordinated. Lanie kept her

There Are No Doors in Dark Places – Page 41

thighs locked together. She could feel whatever was between its legs hurling itself against her.

She felt his potbelly shift. Almost as if there was something inside it.

Its grinning mouth drooled blood over her. She tried to push it away with one hand. The other reaching for the pillow.

"Yuuulllle loovvvve ithh," it whispered.

* * *

The feeder shifted in its cradle. Its glands were already pumping out massive quantities of endorphins and other chemicals to soothe the host and wash away its memories. Spiremes and spiracles wound within the shaft, preparing to invade the host and dismember what it found there. The fetus would be reduced to clumps of cells and chemicals, swallowed back into the body of the feeder for its own sustenance. It would take hours to gorge itself on the unborn.

Other processes were at work. Its chemical factories were manufacturing new hormones manipulate the hosts body. To maintain its chemistry in a state of pregnancy, to generate a false placenta, so that the feeder could return to feed again from rich amniotic fluids and placental blood laden with the chemicals and hormones it needed to survive.

A host could last a feeder years as it slowly withered. The feeder's endorphins would keep it from knowing or resisting until its disintegration had advanced to the point where the host could no longer be said to care, even if it knew what was happening to it.

The feeder was not troubled by the morality of its actions. It was an old race, at least as old as man, and its fortunes had waxed and waned with man's societies. It saw nothing wrong with living off the products of a lesser animal's body, the way man lived on eggs or milk. The world of a feeder was a world of hosts, and manbrains, and cradles. It needed nothing more.

There Are No Doors in Dark Places – Page 42

It wanted the host, and what it carried.

* * *

Lanie grabbed the knife by the blade, her fingers wrapping so tight that she cut herself. She drove the tip of the knife into its shoulder. It arched its back but gave no other sign. Her hand slick with blood, she gripped the handle of the knife and stabbed again, deeper. The thing roared and lifted off her. She pushed it with one hand and stabbed again, this time her knife slid between ribs. It struck at her; she stabbed again, in the neck. A bright arterial spurt of blood splashed across her. Lanie screamed to match its roaring.

It reached for her knife, but seemed to have trouble controlling its movements. It grabbed for her neck instead. She felt its hands like vises, choking her. She stabbed again; her blade went in and caught on the rib. It flung her off the bed.

She caught her hip on the coffee table, he face ground into the floor, catching little pieces of glass and plastic flung by the exploded black and white. She rolled over to keep it in site as she tried to regain her breath, she could barely move.

Barely five or six feet from her, half off the bed, it was convulsing. Jeff wasn't breathing, his eye stared sightlessly. There was no sign of life in his face. But his body convulsed on its back, flopping like a fish trapped out of water. Most horrifying of all, the body still had an erection arching straight up into the air, larger than ever. It seemed to grow.

* * *

The feeder was incensed. The manbrain had lost the host again. The feeder sent monstrous waves of agony up the line, but the manbrain continued to grow less responsive. It ceased to react at all. The feeder was enraged; it explored the connections of their nervous and circulatory systems. The cradle was dying, the manbrain was gone.

There Are No Doors in Dark Places – Page 43

If it had a voice it would have howled. This was not to be borne. The host, it thought, the host had done this somehow. The ingratitude appalled it, it had asked so little, wanted so little from the host.

It was still close by, wet with a luxurious chemical soup, heavy with unborn food/life. The feeder could tell. It was bleeding. The fresh blood excited the feeder; it thirsted for vengeance on the creature that had done this to it. It focused on her.

* * *

The convulsions had stopped. The erection, grown even longer to two and a half, even three feet, had flailed about like some mad serpent.

Then suddenly it stopped. It bent in a gentle arc and then turned to point directly at her. Her blood froze.

Lanie heard a terrible sucking noise. At first she couldn't tell where it came from. Then she realized that the pot belly was moving. By itself. It seemed to twist back, then forth, up then down. The erection bobbed with its motion, but remained fixed on her.

This is a dream. She thought to herself. He raped me and gave me a concussion, and now I'm just laying here and hallucinating.

The corpse's mouth opened for one last small fountain of blood, then the potbelly tore itself free, the skin ripping on and around it. It slid onto the floor between the corpse's legs. A huge shiny pulsing red mound, surrounded by roiling tendrils, with the obscene genitals as its face. It dragged the internal organs of the corpse out with it, and even whole muscles from the arms and legs. Behind it, the skin of the corpse seemed to sag inwards, as if it had been emptied out. The erection had shrunk again, to perhaps two feet, but it had grown heavier, it still seemed to focus on her. It reminded Lanie of a hooded cobra.

With an indescribable wet gurgling noise it dragged itself towards her.

Lanie screamed.

She felt too weak to stand. Terror washed over her. She began to crawl away from the thing, towards the opposite corner of the apartment. To the kitchenette and the bathroom. She thought about crawling into the bathroom, closing the door behind her. She would be safe there. Then she rejected the idea, there was no place to escape from the bathroom. Nothing to defend herself with in there. Lanie imagined the thing forcing its way into the bathroom; herself trapped with the thing. She retched.

The kitchenette, said what little functioning part of her mind remained. There would be weapons in the kitchenette. She dragged herself along the floor. Behind her she could hear the thing following her.

She felt its blunt head stab at her foot as she crawled. But she made it to the kitchenette. Lanie hauled herself to her feet. But it was close behind her. Its tendrils coiled around her legs, pulling her off balance. She fell, taking the cutlery drawer and half the contents of the counter with her.

She threw forks and knives and everything she could put her hands on at it as it humped closer to her, between her legs. They bounced off or penetrated its soft hide, damaging it, but not enough.

The erection drew back into itself. The glans peeled away exposing a structure like a cone of thin strips of coiled red meat.

* * *

The feeder knew it was dying. The corpse's organs trailed out behind it like a bridal train. It knew it would not long survive the death of its cradle. It knew that all it could do was propagate itself. All it wanted to do was invade the host's body, and bury its seed in the unborn life it found inside, so rich, so full of life sustaining nutrients. That would be enough; the seed would reshape the unborn life into cradle, manbrain, and feeder.

* * *

It struck. Lanie caught the shaft of the erection as it lanced toward her, stopping its thrust some four inches from her entrance. It was as thick as a man's fist, and she knew it wanted to go inside her. She sobbed with the effort stopping it cost her. Its strength was appalling, she didn't have proper leverage, and one of her hands was slick with her own blood. In spite of her best efforts the head crept closer to her lips, millimeter by millimeter.

She looked around wildly for something to stop it. There was an oven mitt right beside her. She grabbed for it with her bloody hand. Slowed only by her other hand it thrust wildly forward. She covered herself with the oven mitt. Lanie threw her head back and screamed in agony.

The immense head forced its way into her body for an inch and a half, pushing the oven mitt before it. The ovipositor extruded itself from the center of the shaft. It pressed against the heavy asbestos of the mitten but could not penetrate. The ovipositor retreated back into the shaft with its seed. The shaft gathered itself for another powerful thrust.

Lanie beat at the shaft with her hands. She screamed and scrabbled about wildly for anything to stop the pain. Her hand fixed on a carving knife. Lanie drove the carving knife into the shaft. It convulsed. She screamed and twisted, driving the knife in again and again, sawing until she had it severed. Both ends spouted thick gobs of blood. Her slippery fingers grasped the end of the shaft that had forced its way into her and pulled it out. Only an inch or so, she thought with relief. The pot-belly thing and all its tendrils were limp. It was dead.

Lanie sat there, back propped against the corner of the kitchenette. She swallowed air in great heaping gulps. The apartment looked like a charnel house, blood was everywhere, a corpse lay half on the bed, empty. A thick slug trail of gore lay between the corpse and the thing between her legs. Internal organs trailed from both, and a silver ribbon of intestine joined the two masses. She became aware that there were people hammering on her door.

Let them open the door themselves, she thought.

A new wave of pain passed through her suddenly. Contractions, she realized. She had gone into labor.

She laughed softly. After this, she thought, she could never be afraid of welfare or street people again.

The End

Mister Shepherd

"Lindsey Burnet:" she tapped rapidly, "The hotshot young journalist is the latest and youngest editor to helm the moribund Traders Post, a one sheet rag in a one horse town. Not a mighty flagship but rather a rubber dinghy in the Weston publishing empire.

Trader's Point had been founded in eighteen forty by French missionaries traveling by river. A little farming town had grown up along that lazy stream. Fifty years later the railroad had come through, and the center of the town had moved, like some fickle schoolgirl from the river to the railway. Now, both of its suitors having aged, it hung between them, hugging the road that passed through.

Nestled among lush verdant hills, with an endless stream of clean water, it was a sleepy little farming and service community of a couple of thousand people. A splendid place to raise a family. Or so the chamber of commerce brochure assured her.

"Armpitville," she mumbled to herself, wadding up the pamphlet and throwing it in the garbage. She propped her feet up on her desk and stared sourly at her career.

"Excuse me," Rod said, attracted by the noise.

She looked up at him.

"Nothing Rod," she told him. "I was just thinking out loud. Go back to whatever you were doing."

He disappeared into the back of the newspaper office. Rod was all right. Tall and skinny, he didn't say much. She half suspected he was retarded. She bit her lip for a second, that term wasn't politically acceptable. She needed to be careful, she didn't really care, but it would be awkward if it slipped out unconsciously.

Lindsey put her feet down and turned to her word processor and typed.

"She lords it over one employee and a couple of part timers, in an office that offers both newspaper and print shop services. They told her it was a promotion, as they packed her off to the boonies.

"Promotion or kiss of death? Only time will tell, but in this reporter's humble opinion..."

Irritably she deleted the file. It was time to write a real "introduce the editor" piece. Then on to the court reports. It seemed that someone named Larry Dokes had been charged for the fourteenth time with drunk and disorderly.

"Hello?"

Startled, she looked up.

A tall dark haired man was standing at her desk.

"Did I come at a bad time?" he asked sincerely.

"Oh. No. Not at all."

Lindsey sat upright in her chair and tried to straighten her desk.

"I can deal with whatever you've got right now. Mister..."

"Brentwood. Thomas Brentwood. I'm the principal at the local school."

He offered his hand.

No ring, she noted, as she shook it.

"Lindsey Burnet," she introduced herself, "I'm the new editor here, from out of town."

"Settling into Joe Tighes job, eh? Been here long?"

"Just a couple of days."

He frowned with concern. "Are you feeling all right? You look a little peaked."

Lindsey laughed a little. "I haven't been sleeping too well since I got here. Nightmares or something."

He nodded. "Moving into a new place will do that to you."

"It'll settle down. This seems like a quiet place."

He laughed, "Quiet isn't the word for it."

"Listen," he said, "I just came by to drop off the school calendar and activities. It's a regular feature in the Post. I figured I'd do it in person so I could meet the new editor."

He handed it over; she took it from his hand.

"Well, you've met her. What do you think?"

"I think she'll do a terrific job."

"Thanks."

They smiled at each other for a moment.

They both laughed.

"Well, look," he said, "I think I've got to be getting back to school now."

"Okay."

He hesitated.

"Listen, if you're new in town, why don't you come out and have dinner with me. I'll show you the sights, introduce you to people."

"That would be terrific," she smiled at him.

"Pick you up here, about six?"

"Perfect."

After that, she found herself singing for the rest of the day.

* * *

That evening they had supper at the Charles Diner, the town's one restaurant. After supper they had drinks and flirted, telling outrageous stories about their past love lives.

Afterwards, Thomas took her on a walking tour of the town.

He showed her the old clock tower in Railway Square where peregrine falcons nested. The clock hadn't functioned in twenty years. Occasionally town council would discuss allocating money to have it fixed, but the motion was always voted down on grounds that it would 'disturb the birds.'

They peeked in the windows of the old train station, now the town museum, as he described which artifacts were genuine and which were forgeries.

They strolled past the oversized Imperial Bank building, constructed in an overwrought burst of corporate optimism, and he told her how the Sloane gang had robbed it in the thirties, after spending a weekend at the local hotel. They had been exemplary guests, or so the legend went.

Briefly they looked at the posters for the Marquee, the town's single movie theater and one of the few independents left. Tom introduced her to the owner, Earl Sharp, as he sold tickets in his booth. An old Hitchcock movie was playing. The posters announced a special midnight showing of Bela Lugosi's 'White Zombie.' Earl ventured that he wasn't thrilled with modern films, though he ran them from time to time.

Thomas showed her the local radio tower. A narrow steel framework supported by guy wires, and he related an elaborate story about how a classmate of his had climbed to the top wearing a bedsheet for a parachute and jumped. The classmate had miraculously survived unharmed, until his mother caught up with him...

"So was your mother upset?" Lindsey asked.

"I couldn't sit down for a month," he said before catching himself. They laughed at this little subterfuge.

He showed her the spot Larry Dokes had the car accident that had killed his first wife and child. Larry had never been quite right after that. His second wife had also died. Larry was the town's official black sheep.

"Sounds unlucky," she commented.

Later, when Dokes drove past in his beat up pickup truck, Thomas pointed him out. Dokes was an obese, shaggy, sloppy looking man. He noticed Thomas pointing and waved.

They ambled past rows of well-groomed houses until they came to River Park. She wandered up to a war memorial.

"'The Great War,'" she read out loud, "'in honor of he who brings dreams and nightmares.' What a strange dedication."

"It was from the Voukhours."

"Who?"

"It was this religious sect that settled on the outskirts of town. They sent a lot of sons off to that war. They aren't around anymore, just sort of faded away."

"Really, I've never heard of them."

"Like I said," he told her, "they faded away. You can see the ruins of their old place about a half away. It's very picturesque. In autumn a lot of people like to picnic there. Or make out in the evening."

He put his arm around her waist. It felt very comfortable there.

"What's it look like under moonlight?" she asked.

"Breathtaking."

"I'd like to take a look at it," she said.

"The night is young."

They laughed softly.

They wandered out of River Park and then headed down Dumoulin street.

Dumoulin, he explained, was one of the first settlers, although not the famed French trader. Dumoulin had been blessed or cursed with eleven daughters. Which was why the street had been named after him. No one in town carried the name, although many could trace their ancestry back to him.

"Good evening to you, Tom," a cultured male voice said.

"Good evening, Mister Shepherd," Thomas said amiably. Pleasantly.

"Lindsey, this is Mister Shepherd," Thomas introduced them, "Mister Shepherd, Lindsey Burnet."

"Charmed," he said, taking her hand. His grip was like ice. Poor circulation, she decided. Still, he was so congenial and so distinguished in appearance that she almost curtsied.

He was an old man, somewhere past his sixties, she guessed. With kindly eyes and a shock of white hair. He dressed almost formally, and leaned on a cane he didn't seem to need.

"I'm pleased to meet you," she told him.

"Ah. The new editor at the post. No relation to the entertainer by any chance?" he asked.

"I'm afraid not."

"Mister Shepherd is one of our town's most eminent citizens," Thomas said.

Shepherd laughed softly.

"Such a flatterer this one. Miss Burnet, you'll have to watch yourself with this one, who knows where you might end up."

"I think I can deal with him," she smiled back.

"I'm sure you can. I was just out for my evening constitutional. May I ask?" Shepherd said, politely inquiring of them.

"Oh," said Tom "we were just headed out for the ruins. Lindsey hasn't seen them."

Lindsey leaned lazily against him.

"Capitol," Shepherd said, slapping his hand against his cane. "This is the very best night to view them. Too far for me, alas, but I hope you would not mind if I walked with you a few blocks."

"Of course not," Lindsey told him. "Thomas?"

"By all means."

He beamed at them.

"My thanks. Much as I enjoy these strolls, they can get lonely."

As the three of them walked they chatted softly.

"I've heard your name, Mister Shepherd, but I haven't seen you around before."

"Time is my enemy, Miss Burnet, as it is all of us. I don't get around as much as I used to. I find the bright summer sun particularly troubling. I walk a bit at night, entertain a few visitors, see an occasional movie. It is a subdued life."

"You're quite fit looking for a man your age."

"Ah, flattery. Tom, you may have found a match. Were I but thirty years younger..."

"I'd have no chance at all," Thomas laughed.

"You aren't from around here?" she asked.

"Your subtle ear catches the trace of an accent. Quite right, Miss Burnet, I am not from here, though on some evenings it seems hard to consider I ever existed anywhere else. I'm..."

"What's that?" Thomas said.

There was a pale figure shambling forward under the streetlights. It staggered occasionally as it stumbled. The figure, it was male, wore no pants. Male genitalia drooped, in skin made leprous by streetlight.

It staggered towards them.

"Oh dear," whispered Mister Shepherd.

As he came closer, Lindsey recognized the figure.

"Oh God," she said, Thomas and Shepherd looked at her sharply, "it's the Mayor, Ben Riley. I met him on my first day here."

Thomas and Shepherd stepped forward to greet the stumbling man, each taking him gently by the shoulders.

Mayor Riley's eyes were open and staring. His mouth hung slack, a thick trickle of drool ran down his chin. Dripped onto the road.

"Shit," said Thomas, dancing away for a step.

The Mayor was urinating as he stood there swaying. The bitter fluid ran down his leg and pooled between his feet. He swayed there for a second, wearing nothing but an unbuttoned shirt.

"I fear you've stumbled onto the little skeleton in our closet." Mister Shepherd grinned tightly. "Our Mayor is a somnambulist."

For a second the Mayor's vacuousness seemed to fade enough to register her presence. He clutched at his genitals in a parody of masturbation.

"He sleepwalks," Thomas explained, as they hastily turned him away from Lindsey. She could see the Mayor's shoulder move as his arm beat frantically.

"It hasn't happened in quite a while," Shepherd said, "I hope that this isn't the start of another spell."

"It's early to be sleepwalking," Thomas commented.

"Is he going to be all right?" Lindsey asked.

"Doubtless," Mister Shepherd told them. "There's no reason that you should be inconvenienced this evening. I'll get him home."

"Are you sure?" Lindsey said.

"Perfectly," Shepherd replied, "he'll be no trouble at all. Tom, could I trouble you to stop at the nearest pay phone and tell Elise that I'll be bringing Ben home?"

"Certainly Sir," Thomas answered.

"Well then," Shepherd grunted as he guided the Mayor away, "we'll take our leave. Miss Burnet, I'm sorry we couldn't spend more time."

"Perhaps another time?"

"I will anticipate it with pleasure," he called over his shoulder.

They watched the two of them disappear into the night, before they began walking again.

"Well," Lindsey said after a while.

"I hope you're not going to print this," Thomas said. "Ben is a good man, he just gets his spells."

"REPORTER FLASHED BY ZOMBIE MAYOR," she laughed. "Somehow, I don't think its right for the Post."

He laughed with her, they leaned into each other.

"Actually," he said, "I'm not far from home. I should stop there and phone Elise. Then we can head over to the ruins."

"I have a better idea," she told him. "Let's save the ruins for another night. I'm sure that you can show me lots of breathtaking sights..."

She paused for effect.

"...in your bedroom."

The next few days were very good ones. But the nights were better.

* * *

"Jerry Porter said the strangest thing to me today," she told him.

"Really," Thomas said, "what did he say?"

"I was complimenting him on getting along so well in his wheelchair. He was just handling his disability with good spirits. He looked up at me and he laughed and said, 'glad I'm not a quadriplegic, I'd hate to be boring.'"

"Oh," Tom snuggled up against her, "was that all."

"Isn't that weird though, I mean the attitude that the worst thing about paralysis would be that it would make him dull."

Tom rolled over onto his back.

"It connects for different people," he said. "I get the heeby jeebies just thinking about it."

He rolled onto his side to look at her.

"You know what I mean? I'd hate to be paralyzed. I couldn't stand it. It's my Room 212."

"What?"

"You know," he explained, "in Orwell's Nineteen Eighty Four, it was this room they would take criminals to that contained their greatest fear. I've practically memorized that book."

"Oh," she laughed, "you keep surprising me, I had no idea you were a fan of Orwell."

"I'm full of surprises," he said cattishly, grabbing her. She laughed.

They made sweaty passionate love.

"What's your room?" Thomas asked as they lay back afterwards, sweat drying on their bodies.

"What?"

"You know, from the book."

Lindsey thought for a moment.

"We grew up poor," she said, and licked her lips.

Sensing that there was more to come, Thomas waited.

"Not really poor or anything, we always had enough food and we always had a place to live. Sometimes it was a close shave, but we always got by. We lived in a poor neighborhood, and so we got to see people even worse off than we were..."

"Go on," Thomas said sympathetically.

"Well," she cleared her throat, "there was this old woman. A bag lady, I guess. Not really old. Maybe she was in her forties, but she looked older. She had that leathery wrinkled skin that comes from being out in the sun and the rain day in and day out. Not just that, it was dirty, dirt worked into the grain of her skin like some tattoo or stain. Her clothes were just filthy rags. You could smell her, the staleness. She would come up to you and beg change or cigarettes, sometimes she'd even ask for a beer, and she'd smile while she was doing it. Her mouth would crack open wide, and you'd see she had no teeth, just a...these pink swollen gums."

"Ugh," Thomas said.

"That wasn't the worst," she told him. "She lived in a cardboard box out behind the grocery near our apartment block. It was Pirandello's Grocery. I remember Pirandello, he was a fat jolly man who always had a free piece of candy for a baby. He had this big old mustache, it was like a brush. I used to think he was a pretty nice guy for letting her stay behind his place. I used to think he snuck her food when no one was watching...."

"What happened?" he prompted gently.

"I was coming home from a drama class one night, it was an evening rehearsal actually. I was about thirteen, just starting junior high, just starting puberty. And I turned a corner, there was a short cut home, that took me behind the grocery, and I saw them there. The toothless old bag lady on her knees, her head bobbing on Pirandello's crotch. They didn't see me. I just watched from around the corner until they were finished. Then he gave her a fifth of gin, tucked it back in his fly and went inside.

"After ten minutes, I tried to walk past, but she saw me. She raised her gin bottle and said something. I don't remember what. I just recall her grinning at me and those horrible diseased gums and that tongue flopping between them like a red slug."

She shuddered. He stroked her shoulder comfortingly.

"I was just thirteen, I had no idea what sex was, but watching them, I knew that must be it. What a hell of a first impression, eh?

"Afterwards, I could tell she did it. Not just Pirandello, lots of guys. I picked up these little subliminal cues. Young kids, old men, walking around behind the grocery with brown paper bags or bulges in their pockets. They'd look nervous and focused, like they were ashamed but anxious to do it. Usually booze, liquor or beer. Sometimes food. Once in a while, just some trinket or gift. Yu knew what happened. Nobody'd really notice, unless you were watching for it. It was like I was sensitized, I couldn't help noticing. It really soured me on men for a while, just the idea that they'd go to that. That they would use someone like that, and she'd let them. They were all participating in her degradation, her most of all.

"I used to have nightmares about it."

"About her?"

"About me. I used to have nightmares that I'd turn out like that. Some toothless broken down old whore living in a cardboard box and giving blow jobs to scum for booze...I mean, she was young once. She had her whole world in front of her. What a way to end up."

"Sounds pretty traumatic," he said softly.

"Yeah well," she said, "I think I'm probably over it. I haven't thought about it for years. Maybe it's connected to the nightmares I had when I first came here. I wouldn't have even imagined talking about it. Until now."

"Lyndon Johnson used to have nightmares like that. A lot of people do," he told her. "It's a metaphor for our innate fear of powerlessness. The fear that we'll lose control over our lives, lose our ability to take care of ourselves."

"Fear of falling. Fear of failing," she said, "I guess...you know, I'm a little nervous about this job. Coming here. I'm afraid I might have fallen out of the career loop."

"I doubt it," he said, "a lot of people pass through here. You'll probably transfer out soon enough. Then it's back into the rat race, and I'll lose you to some randy young Turk."

His fingers danced under the covers, skirting the edges of her pubic hair. She giggled uncontrollably.

"I could see some advantages," she breathed, grinning, "to hanging around here for a while."

"Now you're talking," he said, and pulled the sheet over his head as he slid down the bed. Giggling again, she spread her legs.

Later, as she watched him sleep, watched the shadows and moonlight creep over his face; she felt a wave of affection for him. It wouldn't be so bad, she decided, to live here. To surrender to the slow pleasant rhythms of the place.

That night, she slept without nightmares.

* * *

Mister Shepherd was holding court in the diner when Thomas and Lindsey stopped in for a late dinner.

"Good evening Mister Shepherd," Thomas said, bowing his head slightly.

"Good evening Tom, and good evening to you too, Miss Burnet." Shepherd smiled warmly at the couple.

"Miss Burnet, have you met young Mister Sykes?" he introduced them.

A gap toothed teenager wearing a Metallica T-Shirt half got out of his seat to shake her hand.

"Out for a late evening?" Shepherd asked.

"We just thought we'd get something to eat," Thomas explained, surveying the crowded restaurant.

"Well then, tonight you should try the veal, it's in rare form. The salad too is especially crisp, I recommend the house dressing."

"Have you had it?" Lindsey asked.

Shepherd just laughed self disparagingly. "I'm afraid I've an appointment to take my refreshment later. I'm just here to get out of the house and amuse a few friends with fortune telling. I spend too much time in the house."

He shuffled and spread out a line of cards.

"That's an ordinary deck," Lindsey said.

There Are No Doors in Dark Places – Page 61

With a wave of his hand, Shepherd gathered them up, "isn't it? You know, back in the old country I used to use a Tarot deck, but after a while I realized any old deck would do."

He looked up smiling amiably.

"It's just an old fraud," he winked, "like me. But it's still a comforting game, is it not, this illusion of structure and certainty?"

"Now," he said, dismissing them with a wave of his hand, "I have a future to tell. I believe the Petersons are finished, their table should become available so that you do not have to wait."

Further down a man waved for the cheque.

They took the booth a couple of seats down. Shepherd's voice carried as a pleasant wry droning, with occasional snippets of conversation.

Shepherd had been right. The veal was excellent.

The door swung open.

Thomas looked over and quickly ducked his head. He leaned over the table to whisper to Lindsey, "It's Mabel Wertham."

"Who?"

"The town terror, I'll explain later."

Mabel was a heavy woman with mean little eyes buried in a round flushed face. Not grossly overweight, she had rolls of fat over her ankles, and thick stubby fingers like a child's crude drawing of a hand.

She stepped up to the counter and ordered a vinegar special and waited.

"What's a vinegar special?" Lindsey whispered. Thomas shushed her. She looked it up in the Menu.

After a few minutes, Shepherd had finished his reading. As his subject left he stood up to greet Mabel warmly.

"Mistress Wertham," he crooned, pressing his lips to her hand, "I am so pleased you came. Come join me. Perhaps I could read a few cards for you?"

She giggled. Even her giggle had a raucous vulgar sound.

Squeezing into the booth, they exchanged a few pleasantries. Shepherd made cultured, self-effacing jokes. Mabel spoke loudly. Forcefully enough to be heard anywhere in the restaurant. As if in compensation, Shepherd's voice, though not loud, carried similarly effectively.

"I want to know about my daughter," she brayed.

"Certainly," Shepherd said, "Lucy is a fine girl, you must be proud."

"She's a slut!"

Lindsey could imagine the piggy little eyes flashing.

"I have to keep an eye on her all the time or she'd be tomcatting around. She's just a little whore. All girls are these days. No values any more."

Mabel rattled on foully. Shepherd did not speak, but they heard the soft thwack thwack thwack as he laid cards down.

Mabel was going on about blacks and miscegenation.

"Your question?" Shepherd said crisply, interrupting her.

There was a startled pause, as if Mabel was shocked that anyone dared to interrupt her.

Thwack, thwack, thwack.

"There's this black boy that I see hanging around my Lucy. I want to know if she's greasing his pole. Girls these days, they have a taste for black meat. But it's not right. I want to know, because I'll do something about it. You know that you can shoot a black for messing with a white girl, it's a law..."

"Your daughter," Shepherd told her crisply, "is a virgin. The boy you have referred to is Elliot Hawkins; they study together and are good friends. Elliot is a fine boy, one of the best of his generation in this town. Your daughter loves you with her whole heart and without reservation and would do nothing to cause you pain, in spite of how you have treated her. She will be a great comfort to you in the trials ahead. And I'm afraid there will be trials."

"She's a good girl," Mabel agreed sullenly, "but I've had to watch her like a hawk."

Thwack, thwack, thwack.

Lindsey could imagine Mabel flinching at the snap of each card.

"Your husband," Shepherd said simply.

"Carl?"

"Yes, Carl." Thwack, thwack, went the cards. Mister Shepherd didn't even look up. "He is having an affair."

There was a strangled cry.

"With who?"

Thwack.

"He has had many affairs over the years. He began when Lucy was born, when you were sick and in need after having her. He looked to his own needs then. Currently, he is sleeping with Louise Sperling."

"Louise! Louise is my best friend."

Thwack.

"They laugh at you when they are together. He calls you a pig. He tells Louise how you make him sick to his stomach. She takes his organ in her mouth."

"He takes pictures of his women. Lewd pictures of them without their clothes. Exposing themselves. Doing filthy things. He has many pictures.

"Sometimes, at his office, he will lock the door and take out these pictures and abuse himself. He would rather do this than touch you."

There was a dumb animal cry of torment. A beginning of sobbing.

"The pictures of Louise are under the seat of his car."

"What am I going to do?" Mabel wept.

"What has always been done by one scorned. You must revenge yourself upon him."

Thwack.

"Yes," she said, "yes, I will. I'll show him! I'll show them all! He'll pay!"

There were more words. Eventually Mabel stormed out. As the door closed behind her, it seemed as if everyone in the restaurant heaved a sigh of relief.

Lindsey realized she was holding her breath.

"Jesus Christ!" she said.

Thomas looked faintly scandalized.

"Watch your language," he told her.

"What the hell was that?" she demanded.

"That was Mabel Wertham, the town gossip. For years she's been blabbing about what people are doing, making things up sometime. Passing judgement on everyone. I guess it's finally caught up with her. Lucky we were around to witness it."

"It was sick," she said with disgust.

"Mabel? Yeah, I figure she's half psychotic."

"No, I mean that whole scene."

Thomas shrugged. "There's no good way to tell someone that they are being cheated on. Knowing Mabel, if he'd told her in private, she'd have it all over town before the night was out anyway."

"Yeah, but to rub it in like that..."

Thomas laughed softly. "Hell, this is Mabel we're talking about. If she doesn't have details she makes them up. That's got to be tame compared to what she would have come up with."

Lindsey leaned back in her chair.

"You asshole," she said flatly.

"Look," he said equitably, "you're just catching the tail end of a lot of history. Anyway, if you want to be sympathetic to someone, try Carl."

"Carl?" she asked, confused.

"Mabel's husband," Thomas explained, "he's definitely in the wrong there. Mabel may be a psychotic, but she's also his wife. You don't step out. The whole town is going to be behind Mabel. Carl is in for a hard time."

"That's just disgusting," she spat. "This whole place is sick. I want to get out of here."

She started to get up as Thomas protested.

"Jennie," she heard Shepherd call to the young waitress, "come sit with me for a second. Indulge an old man."

He shuffled his cards.

"I have a shift to finish, Mister Shepherd," she stuttered.

He laughed gently. Thwack, thwack.

"I am sure that Mister Tomlin will not mind if you quit your shift early to flirt with a lonely old gentleman."

Thwack.

Nervously she took a seat. Lindsey settled back into her chair, listening. Thomas looked at her sternly.

"This is an important year for you," Shepherd began, "is it not? You graduated this spring, is that right?"

"Yes sir," Jennie replied.

"You have dreams of college, a degree in communications skills. Of travel and fine jobs. These are wonderful dreams."

Thwack. Thwack.

"I've worked hard," she said, "I have really good marks and I have money saved up."

"Armitage college has accepted you into its program. I must congratulate you, Jennie. It is an accomplishment, and we are all proud of you."

Thwack.

"Thank you, Sir," she said.

"But it will not happen," he said.

Thwack.

"What?" Lindsey could feel the tension in the girls strangled gasp.

"I am so sorry, my dear. But you have neither the talent nor the courage. I wish it were otherwise."

"But I'm accepted. I have money," she protested.

"What you lack," he said gently, "is within you. You cannot compensate for your own failings."

"What am I going to do?" she cried.

"Tomorrow evening, after work," he told her, "Larry Dokes will come to pick you up. He will take you to lookout point. There you will drink and mourn your lost future. He will take carnal knowledge of you."

"You promised," she sobbed.

He continued, relentless. "You will become pregnant. But he will do right by you, and take you as his wife."

"You promised I could go to college," she wept.

"Would that you could," Shepherd said gently, "but you must understand that you are not good enough. Try to believe that it is all for the best."

It was enough for Jennie; weeping the girl pulled herself from the booth and bolted from the restaurant.,

"Assholes," Lindsey whispered, rising from the table. Over Thomas's protests she followed the girl out.

"Miss Burnet," Mister Shepherd smiled at her, half rising in his seat.

She snarled wordlessly at him.

"Lindsey," Thomas called.

But she was out the door.

The cool night air was bracing. Lindsey stopped on the steps and looked around. She spotted Jennie marching down Zeller street. She called to her. The girl looked back but didn't stop walking.

"Jennie," Lindsey called again. She raced after her. Halfway there, the girl stopped and waited for her to catch up

"Jennie, you don't know me. My name is Lindsey Burnet."

"You're the new editor of the River Post, from out of town," the girl said. They began to walk.

"That's right. I heard what happened in there."

"So you know," the girl said, flatly.

"Listen Jennie," Lindsey began, "that wasn't right. It's hard enough to get by in the world without people telling you you that aren't good enough. You can't listen to them. You have to believe in yourself."

"Mister Shepherd knows about these things," Jennie said quietly.

"Maybe he does," Lindsey argued, "but that doesn't mean he's right. People told me I'd never amount to anything, but I believed in myself, I wanted to be someone, and I made it. You can make it too. You just have to try."

"You could be right," Jennie said dully.

"You can go to college, if that's what you want. You said it yourself: You have the acceptance; you have the money. Believe in yourself. Do it. I'll believe in you."

Jennie looked up at Lindsey.

"Thank you, Miss Burnet."

"Lindsey."

"Lindsey," Jennie smiled abruptly.

"Listen Jennie," Lindsey offered, "if you ever need help or someone to talk to, or just a friend, come and see me. I've been there."

"I will."

They hugged.

"There you are," Thomas's voice came from behind them. "Lindsey, don't you ever do anything like that again. You embarrassed me in front of everybody, running out like that."

Lindsey released Jennie.

"Gotta go," she smiled, "gotta fight. You get home, and remember: Believe."

Jennie ran off into the night.

Lindsey turned to Thomas.

"I can't believe you..." she snapped.

* * *

It was their first fight. They snarled and yelled at each other until midnight, when they finally made up.

At two in the morning they'd finished making up. They decided that it was so much fun, they'd make up all over again.

* * *

Lindsey slept in to ten o'clock, and woke up to make luxurious love to Thomas as the morning sunlight spilled through the curtains, washing over their bodies.

It was almost noon before she began walking to work, reflecting that she could never have done this in the big city. Small town time was different though. This wasn't such a bad place.

Jennie was waiting for her inside.

"Hello Jennie," Lindsey said, "how long have you been here?"

"A couple of hours," Jennie said.

Lindsey took a seat next to her.

"Sorry to keep you waiting. What can I do for you?"

"You remember last night, when you said if I needed help I should come see you."

"Do you need help?"

"I need to get out of town."

"Okay," Lindsey said softly. "When?"

"Right now," Jennie burst into tears. "While the sun is high and he's weak. I have to get out now, or I'll never get out and I'll be trapped here for the rest of my life!"

There Are No Doors in Dark Places – Page 69

The door to the back room opened, Rod looked out, blankly.

"Please," Jennie whispered desperately.

Lindsey looked up at him.

"It's all right Rod. Jennie here is just a little upset. I'll take her someplace and get her calmed down."

A sudden impulse hit her.

"I may take the afternoon off, Rod."

He shrugged. "Deadline is Thursday," he said, and disappeared into the back.

When the door shut, Lindsey looked at Jennie.

"Are you packed?"

Lindsey indicated a small suitcase beside her chair.

"Where do you want to go?"

"Shawville."

"That's about two and a half hours drive."

"I can catch a bus from there. I'll get to Missionham, get a job. Start college at Armitage in the fall."

"Is this what you really want to do?"

"I have to," Jennie said desperately.

Lindsey licked her lips indecisively. She could get into trouble for helping a minor run off. But she'd been young and desperate herself, once.

"All right then," she said all at once, "we'll do it."

* * *

They were an hour outside of the town limits before Jennie spoke.

"He watched, you know."

"What?" Lindsey asked.

"When I was five years old, and my Daddy came into my room to do things to me at night. He watched."

"Who watched?"

"Mister Shepherd. He'd sit there and watch as my Daddy put his thing..."

There Are No Doors in Dark Places – Page 70

Lindsey reeled with shock. What were the rules about reporting sexual abuse? She wondered.

"He was there when Daddy put the shotgun in his mouth. He came to my room later, and told me exactly what happened."

"I did things for him," Jennie said. The sentences hung there like rotting fruit before suddenly dropping.

"He promised me, I could go to college."

"Mister Shepherd abused you?" Lindsey asked.

"Everybody," Lindsey said. "He's always been around. Some say he was here before the trading post. Before white men came here. Others say he came later passing through, and found he liked it here, and decided to stay. He's real old."

"Jennie..." Lindsey began.

"He takes our blood," Jennie waved her wrist, showing a series of delicate tiny scars. Fang marks.

Lindsey'd seen similar marks on Thomas and thought nothing of them. Everybody has scratches and scrapes growing up.

"But that isn't all. He runs our lives."

Abruptly she turned and looked directly at Lindsey.

"Do you remember when you were a little girl, playing with dolls. Making them dress up, going to tea parties, pretending like they were real?"

"Yes," Lindsey said.

"He's like that. It's like we're toys to him. He decides who we sleep with, and who gets beaten up, and who gets drunk. Who rises and who falls. He gets inside us and feeds all the bad ugly parts, so he can have his little soap operas.

"He lets us dream. He gives us these big dreams, just so he can crush them. Sometimes he drags us down. Sometimes he brings us up. It's like we were a circus.

"We let him. You know that. We let him. We don't think about it. We don't think about where it's going or what happens next. We just do what he wants. Because he makes terrible things happen if you defy him.

"I helped Noreen Hawk give herself an abortion with a coat hanger. I sat there and watched as she bled to death. I sat right next to a phone. I could have called a Doctor. But he didn't want me to.

"That's why I have to get away," Jennie finished her speech with flat indifference.

"Jennie," Lindsey said, "do you know what you're saying? About Mister Shepherd?"

She nodded, stone faced.

"He's a vampire, sucking on the whole town."

* * *

On the way back, Lindsey was profoundly disturbed. Jennie's story was a paranoid's fantasy, of course. The girl was obviously deeply disturbed.

She thought again about those bizarre conversations in the diner. About the way everyone seemed to defer automatically to Mister Shepherd.

She realized that she'd never seen him during the day.

There were no crucifixes anywhere in the town. She hadn't seen a single one. The realization crystallized suddenly in her mind.

There was a church, a drab unassuming whitewashed building at the end of town next to the graveyard. Except for its steeple, it could have been mistaken for a small warehouse.

People didn't even say 'Jesus Christ' in this town. They used worse language. But not that. Forbidden words?

Maybe Shepherd really was a vampire?

If half of what Jenny said was true, he was certainly a monster.

Abruptly, she pushed the idea out of her head. It was too ludicrous to consider.

Lindsey turned on the radio, flipping the dial across until she caught a country music station. She turned it up until raucous twanging filled the air.

Nevertheless, she couldn't get it out of her mind.

In this day and age the classical notion of a vampire, a killer draining one victim dry after another night after night didn't wash. Serial killers were spotted with far fewer victims over a much longer space of time. Society was too tightly woven together, a vampire like that would be spotted and hunted down almost immediately.

But supposing that it didn't kill it's victims. Supposing that a vampire gathered around it a large enough number of people that it could feed regularly without killing. It could just keep moving from one to the other, taking just enough from each one. Like a farmer raising cattle.

But if Shepherd was a vampire, what was she supposed to do about it?

She couldn't very well wander around with a stake and mallet. Where would she get a stake, anyway?

She stopped at a gas station on the way back to fill her tank. As she stretched her legs she noticed that they were having a sale on lighter fluid.

She bought two large cans. They fit into her purse.

Fire destroys vampires, she thought, and then boggled that she would even think of it.

Driving into town, she suddenly thought of the place as a web. A web of petty evil and brutality. And in the center, like some fat spider, sat Mister Shepherd, pulling everyone's strings.

What were the mortal sins? She tried to remember her Sunday school. Sloth, avarice, envy, greed, gluttony... The truly deadly sins, because every evil act could be traced back to their impulses. There was certainly enough of it in this town.

And in every other town, she told herself, struggling for rationality.

There doesn't have to be a prince of evil to make fathers molest their daughters.

Lindsey found herself driving down Center Street, turning up onto Traders Avenue.

There was Mister Shepherd's house. It was a quaint old three story construction, bright yellow, a baroque assembly of eaves and gables covered with rust brown shingles. Its windows shone in the fading daylight.

She parked in the driveway.

There was at least an hour of sun left, she decided.

Lindsey walked around to the back. Mister Shepherd was one of the town's leading citizens. It would be worthwhile interviewing him for the Post. And she should apologize for running out of the restaurant like that.

She would knock on the door and find Mister Shepherd sitting in his kitchen, enjoying the afternoon light, reading a book or having tea. He'd invite her in and they'd have a nice little chat, and the spell would be broken.

And she'd never admit to anyone, not even Thomas, that she'd even half believed Jennie's story.

She looked at the windows. They weren't.

That is, they had been windows, and certainly looked the part. But now she could see that where the panes of glass should be, was only brightly painted wood, with a layer of plastic sheeting to shine in the illusion of glass. You couldn't see through them.

Sunlight couldn't get in.

Lindsey shivered.

She climbed up the back porch and raised her hand to knock. She decided not to. Carefully she tried the back door. It wasn't locked.

She slipped inside.

Isn't this what they do in bad movies, she wondered.

The kitchen was dusty and dank, lit only by a forty watt bulb. There was a stench in the air, as of meat rotting. She checked the fridge. Nothing. She opened the cupboards. Empty.

Did anyone live here?

Moving as quietly as she could, she stepped into the hallway. It too was dimly lit. There was a broken chair at one end. Yellowing piles of old newspapers and magazines sat precariously upon it.

Lindsey held her breath, listening.

Nothing.

She ventured down the hallway, glancing into the side rooms.

Lindsey stepped into the living room, and there it was in the faint electric light.

A coffin.

All right, she decided, check and see if he's in there, and this is for real. Then soak it with lighter fluid and walk away. An old house like this would go up like a torch.

She stepped forward.

There was a sudden sharp pain in her temple. She felt herself falling bonelessly to the floor. As her body rolled to the side, the last thing she saw was Larry Dokes grinning down at her.

Blackness.

* * *

"Miss Burnet," Mister Shepherd said genially, "I'm so glad you chose to drop by."

Lindsey struggled to focus her eyes. There was a throbbing pain in the side of her head and a sticky wetness at the edges of her left cheek and down her neck. The coffin was open, Shepherd was sitting up in it.

There Are No Doors in Dark Places – Page 75

Behind him, to the sides were other men, smiling gently. She made out Thomas and Larry Dokes and Mayor Riley.

It's night out, she thought, he's up. Adrenalin surged through her, followed by the desperate will to believe that this was all a practical joke. That any minute now they could all burst out laughing. Her will to believe that, to clutch at any alternative, was almost palpable.

"I know," Shepherd said, as he climbed out of the coffin, "silly isn't it? A bed would be so much more comfortable. Even a nice couch. But this seems so appropriate."

He chuckled self-effacingly.

"I guess I've just seen too many movies."

"Uhh," she moaned softly. She couldn't move her head. Not more than a centimeter or two. She couldn't move at all she realized. She was splayed forward like a paralyzed skydiver, her knees barely an inch above the ground, arms outstretched, in some sort of metal bracing.

Fear of falling, she thought.

"Have you seen Bela Lugosi's films? The man was a genius. Even in utter crap he stood out, he was just so much better than anyone else around him. I'm not ashamed to say I feel influenced by him."

Behind her a door opened and closed. She heard footsteps.

Shepherd looked up and smiled.

"Hello Malcolm," he said.

"Sorry I'm late," a gruff voice said nervously, "Katie had to wait for the roast before she could take over at the pumps."

"It's all right Malcolm," Shepherd told him graciously, "Miss Burnet was just coming around."

He looked at her.

"Or should I say, 'Ms Burnet.' I know how people are about their appellations. I'd hate for you to feel I was treating you without due respect.

"You did, after all, take the role of fearless monster slayer."

He bent down until he was at eye level. He had red burning eyes she noticed. When he spoke, his breath carried a terrible stench.

She couldn't speak. Words died in her throat, rather than coming out to face the monster. Suddenly, she had a terrible conviction that he had chosen her for that role, that he'd orchestrated this evening.

That she was here because he'd planned it all along.

And he'd already planned whatever came next.

"Perhaps I could call you Lindsey," he said, he smiled showing yellowed fangs, "I'd like that."

"Lindsey," he addressed her, "you've been led astray about me. I'm not your enemy. I'm not anyone's enemy. The people here can testify to that."

There was a chorus of 'yeah's and 'yes's' in the room around her.

"I'm not evil. You shouldn't even be thinking of evil. Good and evil are archaic concepts, flawed from the very beginning. You might as well believe in Plato's notions of ideal forms.

"I don't make people do things, or force them into despicable acts. It's not like that at all. I'm not a puppet master.

"People are just people. That's all. They are just tangled webs of needs and desires, urges and impulses covered by a veneer of rationality. Bundles of internal drives that lead them to compassion and cruelty, struggling to make choices in life. Difficult choices, easy choices, altruistic choices, selfish choices. Any kind of choice, really."

He shrugged.

"Do you know what frightens people? Fear of falling? Fear of failure? Those are just part of it, avatars to the real fear. What people are really afraid of...is the unknown. They are afraid of all the maybes in their lives. Even the worst certainty is better than the yawning unknown.

"All I do is provide order; I give people a framework to live their lives through. People want security in both the good things and bad things that happen to them, or in the things that they do to each other. Someone to give them permission, to guide them, I give that to them.

"The law tries to do that, tries to provide structure, to order people's lives. But it's hopelessly mired in the concept of trying to make people be good, rather than just ordering their lives as people.

"Rape and murder. Child abuse and lynching. Heartbreak and violence. Love and jealousy and passion. It would all happen without me. In other places it does happen without me. In fact, much worse things happen. At least here, from me, there is comfort and freedom.

He grabbed her face between two elongated fingers and twisted it painfully.

"Look at Tom," he said. "I don't make Tom do anything."

"Course not," Tom said amiably.

"If I suggested Tom perform an unnatural act on Larry Dokes..."

Larry grinned wildly as Thomas went down to his knees and began scrabbling at his crotch. Lindsey's eyes blurred with the beginning of tears as she heard the sound of a zipper being pulled. She felt her gorge rising in horror, on the verge of vomiting.

"Uh uh," Shepherd warned her, twisting her face back to look at him. He ran a finger of his free hand down the side of her cheek and they looked at it. Red and sticky. Thoughtfully he put it in his mouth and sucked it.

"I have tasted of sorrow and laughter, despair and love. I have supped from pregnant women and old men, newborn babes and pubescent boys. I have savored all the thousand flavors of the human condition," he said reflectively. "But it's already there, all those secret filthy impulses, I do not manufacture it.

"I simply guide it. Allow it expression. In their hearts, I'm what they want.

"If Tom were to do such a thing as I describe, it would be because he wanted to, not because I made him. Isn't that right Tom?"

Thomas mumbled his gurgled assent, face buried in Larry's crotch.

Shepherds face broke into a hideous grin.

"You see. And if Larry were to have an accident..."

She heard Tom gasp and pull away with a gurgling laugh, heard a soft hiss and caught an acrid scent that she associated with urination.

"...it's just two good old boys having some fun," Shepherd concluded. He winked.

"I'm not some wolf from the forest, some ravaging wild beast tearing through victims.

Shepherd glanced away briefly and cleared his throat.

"Tom, do you have something for us?" he asked.

Hastily Thomas climbed to his feet.

"Oh yeah," he said with embarrassment, "I almost forgot, I have it here."

From the corner of her eye she watched him pull an object wrapped in white cloth from a back pocket. He handed it to Shepherd who accepted it graciously.

"Thank you Tom, don't worry about it, you can go back to whatever you were doing."

There Are No Doors in Dark Places – Page 79

Tom sank back to his knees, happily. Secure in Shepherd's will.

Shepherd kneeled before her, carefully unwrapping the white cloth.

"Try to understand, Lindsey. These people love me. They are my flock, all of them.

It was a pair of pliers.

"And you will be too."

She started to scream.

* * *

Jennie walked across the uneven linoleum, gripping the edges with her toes. There was a kind of pleasant sensuality to it.

Barefoot and pregnant, she thought, that's me.

She ran a hand protectively across her swollen belly. She was going to have twins. Shepherd promised. Two healthy beautiful boys. She flushed with pride.

Larry must have felt it too. Sometimes, when they were in bed together, he would just lay his head against her stomach and listen to them kick. He hardly used her in that way, anymore. And he never hit her in the stomach these days. Just in the face and the arms.

Through her good eye, the other had swollen shut yesterday, she watched Larry plough through his supper. He ate with distracted gusto. Abruptly he finished and stood up.

She moved to take his plate as he strode towards the refrigerator. Throwing it open, he grabbed a half empty bottle of Jack Daniels and headed to the back door.

"Going out with the boys," he told her.

She watched him leave, with a smile distorted by her split lip. He'd be gone for a while, she knew, and Thomas would come over.

Shepherd had given her Thomas to make her feel like a woman. Thomas would comfort her and care for her. He'd promised her that Larry wouldn't ever find out. She didn't think the babies were Larry's. Maybe she would ask Shepherd about it someday.

Life was good.

* * *

In the fading light of the dying sun, Larry pulled his truck up beside the Safeway and stepped out. Flies buzzed around him, he waved them away irritably.

There was no one around. He took a few steps towards the dumpsters and shook his whiskey bottle. The sound of the sloshing carried through the evening stillness.

"Come on out Girley," he called softly. "Big daddy got a present for you."

From behind the dumpsters Lindsey crawled from her cardboard lean-to shelter, grinning and slobbering toothlessly.

The End

Fighting the Beast

Saul's day shift was over and it was time to go home. He walked out of the factory past the watchful eyes of the guards in their towers. As always the back of his neck itched as he imagined their scopes sighting on him. It was the badge, of course. The yellow star on the armband that he was never allowed to take off.

He sat alone in his designated bus shelter beside a picture of the Leader. The omnipresent loudspeaker blared promises and exhortations, predictions of eminent victory. There were other people in the shelter, but they stood away from him. They had stood away for years, resolutely refusing to recognize his presence. His armband took him out of the category of 'People.' Deep down inside him, something snarled in misery and rage and clawed at the bars of his soul.

The bus arrived; it bore little resemblance to the buses of his childhood. Unpainted, the silver rivets of its armor plating stood out in stark relief, the bulletproof glass of the windows were covered by heavy wire mesh. At the front and back were tractor lines and winches to pull the bus if it became stuck. At the top were bubble turrets, and the air intakes which would allow the bus to drive through up to eight feet of water.

He remembered driving in cars with his father, but cars had become an expensive and fatal luxury. He thought often of his father. He remembered how his father moaned as he died; how he had reached up to hold Saul as his ruined heart spasmed for the last time. He remembered the men with guns who stood around him as he wept for his father.

"G'day Saul," said the first guard as he got on the bus.

Each bus had two guards in addition to the driver. They stood in glistening silver cages that reached to the bubble turrets. He didn't know the rear guard, but he had become almost friendly with the front man. His name was Winston, he was an expatriate Australian. The Leaders broadcasts assured the nation that there was still an Australia. Winston didn't know, and hardly cared, he would never be able to go back.

"Hello Winston." The guards preferred that their names not be used, but Saul clung to the vestiges of human contact. "The usual seat?"

Winston nodded. Saul took his usual seat opposite the guard cage, away from the sealed driver's basket. Winston cocked his rifle and took his usual aim at Saul's heart.

There was a radio speaker on the bus, of course. The Leaders latest live speech had finally droned to an end and the international news came on. The major story was the ongoing success of the fifth aid mission to India. The four previous missions to India had been ongoing successes as well, and they had all vanished without a trace. There would be reports on Europe, Africa, Latin America. Saul often thought that the media carried so many international stories to demonstrate how comparatively well off the nation was.

Crossing one of the many barren stretches, they passed another bus lying on its side by the road. Its armor and turrets had done little good; something had picked it up and opened it, like a child shelling a pea pod.

Nobody commented on it, it wasn't a safe thing to do. By tomorrow it would be hauled away. Saul hoped that the flying gun ships would track down whatever had done it. Soon after that they passed through a group of Zombies.

They must have been drawn to the road by the sound of traffic. Zombies were slow and unintelligent, motivated only by dull hunger. The driver ran down the few that made it onto the road without changing speed. Saul imagined that he could feel the lurch and squish as the heavy wheels ground under what had once been human flesh and bone. The rear guard squeezed off a half dozen shots at the remainder. Some of the ones that fell didn't get up. Winston's rifle sights never moved from Saul.

Back in the beginning, Zombies had been a major problem because of their sheer numbers. Today, they had been reduced to the status of bad omens and harbingers of far more terrible things. Still, they held an unhealthy fascination for many people.

They were coming to the Troll booths that marked the boundaries of the Industrial City. The driver stopped briefly, passed his chit and waited for the gate to rise. Saul could see the Troll crammed into the Tellers cage. It was huge and grotesque. Its fundamental repulsiveness was incongruous with the neat overalls and golden armband it wore. As if it needed an armband, Saul thought. He almost laughed.

So many people had been lost in those first desperate years after The Balance Had Shifted, so many more had died.

That was how most people thought of it: The Balance Had Shifted, in serious capital letters. Somewhere, somehow, THE BALANCE HAD SHIFTED.

In a struggle between warring forces/beings something had gained an advantage and something else had lost it, and the struggle continued. A darkness came into the world.

People had changed, things changed. There had been no rhyme or reason to the change. The dead rose to walk the earth, full of mindless, avaricious, hunger. Some good men changed into monsters, while some bad men remained human. Children turned into Goblins, lawyers became Vampires, and nobody had a word for what many politicians had turned into. Whole villages had changed while their neighbors were unaffected. Prisons transformed into

There Are No Doors in Dark Places – Page 85

abattoirs, as those who changed turned on those who, unaccountably, had not.

Stones had talked and trees had walked. Metals and crystals had taken on new properties. The physics of the world were subtly different. Sometimes Saul wondered if the earth still moved around the sun, or if that too had changed.

The bus bounced and lurched on its way. The radio blared the news that everywhere the forces of darkness were being driven back. A cure was about to be discovered. A battle about to be won. And then it reeled off the latest list of curfews, proscriptions and shelters. The list of shelters was always slightly different, a few new ones added, some old ones gone. There were fewer shelters than last year. Last year had fewer than the year before. Saul found it difficult to see this as a good sign.

The radio finished its messages and then began its recitals from the Holy Books. Religion, any religion, offered a weapon against the dark creatures, but it wasn't always a reliable weapon. Vampires did not always flinch from the crucifix, for instance. Indeed, some of the dark creatures laughed at it when it seemed strongest.

The dark creatures didn't appear to understand the situation any better than the survivors. They didn't know why the Balance had Shifted, or what/who it shifted for.

In those first desperate years, so many people had changed, and so many more died, that the machineries of civilization had almost stopped. The wheels had squealed and the gears had ground, each lost soul like a particle of grit. Civilization, choked with death, had moaned and shook and almost seized up like an overheated motor.

Some of the dark creatures could be trained, or reasoned with, could be responsible. They helped to fill the gaps in a society that had found itself with too many needs and too few bodies. But, they could not be trusted, not completely.

Far too many of the dark creatures could not be trained. Too many could not be trusted or reasoned with. Creatures that could shell an armored bus like a peanut. Deep down inside him, the Beast, sensing the approaching night, growled and roared.

They were approaching his building now. He thought of his wife and his children. He thought of Mister Chang, his neighbor down the hall. Chang had been gone three days now, he was due back tonight. If he came back.

Still, the industrialized democracies had coped. They had rocked and shuddered and eventually righted themselves. The third world hadn't. India and China had exploded into chaos and then broke into hundreds of fragments. One by one their lights had gone out; now all that came out of India was an occasional desperate distress call.

Sometimes people whispered that the dark creatures had won in India. That they had won here. That the Leader was a puppet, and all the fortresses were just cages and larders for luncheon meat, kept passive by an illusion of independence.

Whispers like that would earn you a bullet in the back of the brain. If it was true, it was not the kind of truth that could be told.

The bus halted in front of his building. It was a prison-like structure, with barred windows and heavy stone construction. Its surface was dotted with formidable hex signs. There was a two story portrait of the Leader beside the gatekeepers post. The way looked to be clear. He waited until the other passengers had departed before he got off.

"G'night Saul, stay human."

Deep down inside him the Beast gibbered and howled, thrashing at the bars of its cage, hungry for blood.

"Good night Winston, stay human," he said. It was almost a private joke between them.

He walked up the stairs. Nobody used elevators anymore. Too much risk of being trapped with something coming to get you. Or worst of all, trapped with something in there with you.

He thought he heard scattered machine gun fire from the roof. Night was when they were most active, but twilight was sufficient for the early risers. There were even a few that walked out in the sun.

He walked down the empty hallways. The walls were lined with patriotic slogans and protective symbols. Every door was locked, barred, and bolted, yet he knew that eyes watched warily from keyholes as he passed. At the end of each hallway a security camera monitored all movement.

They all knew him. Two years ago, there had been a petition to have him expelled from the building.

Finally, he reached his own door. He knocked and waited. He heard the sound of bolts being drawn and the door opened. Saul stepped inside and embraced his wife. Sharon had lost weight but her small frame fit inside his arms as if they had been made to be together. Her hair, once smooth and lustrous, was now knotted and straggly. The last few years had been hard on her and it showed in the lines of her face. But Sharon was still beautiful to him after all these years.

He could feel it, through the holster she wore; through the steel chambers of the gun. He could feel the silver. By law she could never take off the gun while he was around.

But he didn't care. He was holding her and he loved her. For just a moment the relentless misery of his life dimmed.

Ross was in the apartment. Saul's small pleasure went sour. Ross was the man with the manacles. The man who, for seven days each month, put him in the cage in the basement. That it was necessary didn't matter; Saul still could not like the man.

His son was watching "Save Your Life" on the television. "Real Heroes" was coming on soon, but Saul had the impression that his son was surreptitiously paying more attention to Ross than the television.

"It's not time," Saul said, staring at Ross.

"I know," Ross answered. "It's Chang. We think he's coming back tonight. We'd like you to be there."

"Leave me alone. You know I'm not allowed to so much as hold a weapon."

"That's true," agreed Ross, "but you can smell them and we'd appreciate the warning."

"Do I have a choice?" Saul asked.

"Sure," answered Ross, "You can go in the cage. If Chang is coming back we don't want him calling you up behind our backs."

Resentment flickered deep inside him. The Beast caught it and fanned the spark, nurturing a flame. It growled.

They didn't say much on the way to Chang's apartment. Ross walked behind him all the way. Misses Chang and her two children met them at the door. There were five men inside. They were part of the buildings militia, a resurrection squad.

He noted the Smith & Decker Crossbows, the barbed rosewood quarrels and rosewood stakes. Crucifix hammers and garlic ropes hung in easy reach. Each carried a flask of what must be Holy Water, each smelled vaguely of garlic. The only man who wasn't tricked out in a resurrection kit was Ross. Ross had a gun. The gun had silver bullets.

"Do you have to keep the kids here?" Saul asked.

One of the men sniggered. Saul recognized Malcolm.

"It's 'because they always come after family first. But who knows which family member?" Malcolm said.

"I thought you'd done this before," another man said. He was short and piggy, from another part of the building.

"I've done it," Saul answered.

He remembered hammering the stake into his father, his father screaming, tears running down his own face. The other members of the Resurrection Squad standing back. He had been human then. The Beast had come into his life two years later. He hated the piggy little man.

The Beast caught the hatred as it flew by, stoked it, and added it to the fire it was building. The night was coming on and it was getting stronger.

Misses Chang served him tea. It was hot and strong; he bowed gratefully and sat down. The apartment was furnished in a Spartan oriental manner. He liked it. He wished that he had gotten to know the Changs a little better.

"How do you know he is coming back? Maybe something just ate him and that's it." Saul asked.

"We've rolled the bones and rolled the stones on this one. Lots," Malcolm told him, "the signs say he's getting up and coming back tonight."

"Do the signs say I'm supposed to be in it?"

"Your sigils are linked," Ross said. Ross was still behind him. Ross would probably stay behind him.

Somehow dark creatures could sense each other. Often they seemed to work or act together, and the presence of one would often act as a trigger for the black potential in others.

"So maybe you're going to kill two monsters?"

"We rolled the stones," said Malcolm, noncommittally.

Saul felt the circle tightening around him. Deep down the Beast felt it too and tested the cage.

They passed the time, waiting.

"What's it like?" a man asked, Saul recognized Rick. His son, full of youthful enthusiasm, knew the entire resurrection squad by heart. Pictures, names, families, apartments. Saul hadn't been interested, but some of it must have rubbed off.

For a second Saul didn't know what he meant.

"You live with it." Saul told him. "It's in you all the time. You can feel it watching you. It wants to get out."

Suddenly, he felt a need to talk about it.

"Most of the time I keep it in, sometimes it gets strong and it gets out. Full moons and things like that. But it's always inside, always watching and waiting."

He drew a breath.

"It sleeps with me. Did you know that?"

Of course they didn't. He could feel a deadly silence from Ross, who sat behind him.

"When it first came, I was afraid to go to sleep. I thought it would get out then. I stayed awake for six days, until I got so groggy that it got out anyway. But all it wanted to do was sleep. It sleeps when I do, you see."

He laughed.

"My wife tells me that sometimes when I'm sleeping I get furry."

He felt it then. Like an insects foot on a spiders web. A vibration like a guitar string being strummed.

"It's here!" he said.

Galvanized, they brought up their crossbows and swept the room. The Vampire had appeared like a gust of foul wind. Before anyone could react it had its fangs in Misses Chang's neck.

Rick was closest; he stabbed with the rosewood stake. The Vampire, Chang, snapped his back with a spinning kick, refusing to let go his prey. Rick went flying, his body cartwheeling in a sickening arc. The children were screaming. The Vampire was still holding Misses Chang; her feet off the ground when crossbow bolts were loosed.

They tore through the air, with an awful thudding noise; they embedded in Misses Chang's body. She didn't make a sound. The Vampire screamed, a sound like bones being splintered; and hurled Misses Chang. The body struck the wall and fell limp; Saul could hear her bones snapping.

Saul rocked back and forth. His face was hot and flushed and his ears were full of the Beasts roaring. It was pushing its way up. He fought it, but it was pulling him down.

The scene was breaking down to a collage of images and sounds without meaning. The men of the resurrection squad shouting. The Vampire charging. The children were trying to drag their mother's body out of the apartment. Quarrels blurred through the air. The Vampire gracefully swept up a small table to catch them. It kicked and thrust with blinding fury, snapping a crucifix in two.

Some distant part of his mind noted that Chang, at some point in his life, must have studied martial arts. The skill had returned after his death like some witches gift. And then the red roar of the Beast drowned all thought.

Ross was in front of the children. He raised his gun; the Vampire straight armed him, snapping the bone. Ross almost collapsed, but grabbed the Vampire in a death grip. The creature lurched off balance. Slavering, it dug its fangs into Ross's shoulder.

The thing was almost on top of the Beast. The undead putrefaction of the Vampire filled the beast's nostrils. The beast snarled, flecks of foam spraying from its muzzle. Chang growled, the blood bubbling around Ross's shoulder where he refused to let go. He flicked a couple of stiff fingered blows at the Beast. The first penetrated the Beasts right eye, it growled and leaped. Deep inside Saul screamed at the pain.

They tore three fingers from the Vampires hand. Reflexively the Beast tried to swallow but its body rejected the undead flesh. It spat. Almost instantly, Chang was on it like a whirlwind, a volley of kicks and blows shattered the Beasts bones. They knit almost instantly, but the pain forced the Beast to all fours.

The Vampire turned back to the children. Saul, floating in the sea of pain, saw this from the Beasts remaining good eye. An image of his own wife and child flashed though his mind. Not the children, he thought formlessly.

Never the children. He dug his mind into the Beast and drove it up.

The Beast lunged. The undead tried to meet the leap but the Beast caught it as it turned. Slavering jaws tore into the Vampires face, claws ripped into its belly, leaving yellow pus trails that closed up an instant later.

The fiends roared and tore at each other, biting and kicking and clawing relentlessly. Where the Vampires teeth rended the beast's hide, its flesh bubbled and rotted and fell away. But always their wounds healed and closed and knitted instants after the wounding.

The Vampire tore its way deep into the Beasts abdomen. Pain saturated the Beasts mind. Saul held onto the Beast in his mind, forcing it to attack. With a convulsive wrench, the Beast snapped the Vampire's spine and hurled it the length of the room.

A second later the Beast was on top of it. For a second their eyes met. The Beast looked into the cold, intelligent, darkness of the Vampire and felt its mad power subsiding. Through the fading Beast, Saul looked into the Vampire.

Bile rose up in his soul. The cold darkness of the Vampire seemed to contain all the misery of the past years. The loneliness, the fear. The pain of carrying the Beast for every waking moment of his life welled up inside. Feeding all the pain and madness of his life into the Beast, they leapt together.

Powerful jaws sought the Vampires neck, began to draw together. The Vampire struggled in his grip. It clawed at the muzzle, grasping, trying to pull the jaws apart. But its maimed hand betrayed it. The Beast felt the cervical vertebrae between its teeth. With a convulsive twist, the head tore free, bouncing across the apartment, like a grotesquely painted ball.

The Beast rolled off onto its back. Agony screamed through its mind like rockets streaming red trailers. Its body struggled to heal its wounds. Saul moaned. As the flesh shifted and rippled in alternating waves of pain, he could no longer tell himself from the Beast.

The Vampires body thrashed erratically. He/They were vaguely aware of someone driving a stake into its heart with their bare hands.

His, the Beasts, body arched. He drew in great racking breaths. He twisted onto his side, curling into a fetal position. He wept a torrent of painful sobbing.

He became aware of his wife's presence, holding her gun. He reached for her with one trembling limb. His hand clasping hers felt the gun. Through blurring eyes, he watched her, watching his hand. He watched the changes ripple across it over and over. Flesh and fingers, fur and claws, flesh then fur.

His wife was weeping too. Poor Sharon, he thought.

Sweet silver, he thought, set me free. He pulled the gun until its muzzle lay against his forehead.

"Please," he begged.

But she couldn't. She held him and cried with him for his pain as the Beast howled inside and the changes swept across his flesh. She loved him.

The End

Allison

It was a hot June day and the sun had that scorching too bright quality that only comes on the bowels of summer when the heat is suffocating and bottomless, without beginning or end.

The door was open. The officer could smell blood in the hallway. He couldn't see any from where he stood. But the smell of blood seemed to fill the hallway, a physical presence even from where he stood. It was a thick, rich, burned metal smell that gorged his nostrils.

He stood in front of the door. Just as he was about to knock, he abruptly changed his mind. He moved to the side of the door, undoing the buckle of his holster.

He reached over and knocked.

He waited.

Nothing. Nothing but the smell of blood.

He listened carefully. There was a television set on inside, playing softly. Nothing else.

Experimentally, he tried the handle.

It turned.

He pushed the door wide open.

There was a whiff of rancid blood smell, pungent in the heat.

Carefully, he entered; one hand on the gun in its holster. But not quite holding it.

Down the apartment hallway there was a motorized wheelchair, in a corner and close to the wall so as to be out of the way.

Heart pounding, he moved forward. He turned toward the living room.

There was a man sitting in the easy chair, watching television. He glanced up at the Officer. He appeared to be late thirties, in good shape, with that intense groomed look you found sometimes in yuppies or born again Christians.

He looked very tired.

There was blood on him. Dried blood, on his hands, on his shirt, smeared in the lines of his face.

The Officer had a momentary image of the man rubbing his temples, his cheeks, in exhaustion. With bloody hands.

There was a book in his hands, the pages stamped with bloody thumb prints. The Officer could just make out the name; it was an old, well-worn paperback copy of "Why Bad Things Happen to Good People."

The television was playing a soft sell evangelical program.

The phone sat beside the easy chair. It was smeared with blood.

The Officer stepped into the living room, standing beside an old fashioned glass cabinet. There were trophies in it, Women's tennis, by his glance, they were in beside framed photographs: Of a women with a tennis racket, of the woman with the man, a grinning couple, of the woman running in a marathon crowd. The Officer barely noted them.

"Did you call us?" the Officer asked, "Did you call the police?"

"Yes."

It had been over an hour ago. The message had been ambiguous. Intake had assigned it a low priority. Just one officer dispatched, eventually.

The apartment reeked of blood.

The Officer was starting to feel that they'd made a mistake.

The man in the chair seemed apathetic.

"What's your name?" the Officer asked softly, advancing to crouch beside the seated man.

There was no response.

"What's your name?" he asked again.

"John," the man said, softly.

"John," the Officer repeated. "All right, John. John, are you injured?"

John shook his head, softly, not looking at the Officer.

"What happened, John?" the Officer asked.

John's lips moved, but no words came. He stared at the television set. One eight hundred numbers marched across the bottom of the screen.

The Officer took the remote control from John's lap and hit mute. The silence was claustrophobic. Between the pungent reek of blood and the cessation of noise, the Officer felt his heart begin to pound.

"John?" he whispered self-consciously.

"What's your name?" John asked.

"Constable David Bayer."

"Have you been a police officer long, Constable Bayer?"

"Long enough," the Officer replied. Four years.

"Are you married?"

"Yes."

"Do you love your wife?" John asked, and then, without waiting for a reply said, "My wife's name is Allison."

A look of pain passed over him, his brows knit and eyes crinkled and for a second, the Officer thought he was going to burst into tears.

"Was Allison," he corrected.

A sudden flush went through the Officer, making his cheeks burn. Embarrassment at seeing the emotion, or perhaps a moment of inspiration.

"Something happened to Allison?" he prompted.

Again, the sudden wave of anguished contortion swept over John's features.

"October," he whispered. He seemed to be drifting into memories. "She ran the Boston Marathon two years ago, did you know that? She was planning on doing it again, until the accident."

"John," the Officer said firmly, "is that Allison's blood?"

John looked at his hands.

"John?" the Officer prompted.

"Mostly," John said. "Mostly Allison's."

He seemed to think it over, "All Allison's. All hers."

"John," the Officer said, "what did you do?"

John shrugged, seeming lost and small.

"Nothing. I came home."

A break in then? Some sort of disturbance? Possible suicide? Or he was lying? Waiting for his chance?

"John, where is Allison?"

"In the kitchen."

The Officer shifted position, drawing his weapon. He didn't know why. He just wanted it to make him feel better.

"John? All right, John. I'm going to go look in the kitchen. But I want you to stay right here. Don't move. Will you do that, John?"

No answer.

John just kept staring at the television.

Finally, he nodded.

"I'm going into the kitchen, John. Stay right where you are, all right?"

The Officer padded toward the kitchen. There were footprints. Bloody footprints in the carpet. Only one set. They lead out of the kitchen towards John.

With each step he took, the sick reek of old blood became thicker. He breathed through his mouth, but he could still feel it at the back of his nostrils, catching in the top of his throat. His eyes watered.

He stood in the kitchen doorway.

Allison sat in the corner, her back leaning against some cabinets. Her head was up, she looked almost alive.

Her belly had been carved open.

There was a butcher's knife clenched in her hand.

For a moment, the Officer couldn't breathe.

"Jesus," he whispered. "Jesus, Jesus, Jesus."

News reports of psychotic women so desperate for a child that they'd carved open pregnant women to steel their babies flipped through his head.

He forced himself to stare.

There was a pool of blood covering almost the whole floor.

He'd never understood the term before. The blood hadn't just covered the linoleum. It obliterated it. It sat there, a featureless shining flat liquid surface giving no sign of anything beneath it. A red sea, a dark pool of terrible infinite depth.

Here and there it had been smeared and you could see the linoleum underneath. The blood was disturbed, footsteps, smearing and slipping in, then out.

The smell of blood was overpowering. A live smell turned to death. The Officer remembered how his nose had been broken in little league and how it had filled with blood. He remembered the thick pungent scent.

This was worse. This was old blood, turning bad, turning decayed and sour, filling his nostrils. How could a simple human being contain such a dark immensity?

He stared at the woman.

She was naked, blood caked skinny legs sagging muscle. Blood and gore had run copiously down the gaping wound of her belly, down between her thighs, until it seemed there was nothing left there but a matted clot. Blood had soaked her arm, the one holding the knife. There was some on her other hand, but smeared, as if she'd used that hand to investigate the wounds. The fingers still clutched a loose fold of skin.

Self-inflicted?

Her stomach had been excised. She'd cut desperately and wildly, slicing herself open with a dozen clumsy cuts. She'd gouged deeper with increasing care, stabbing and severing organs and intestines, until finally neatly the uterus had been sliced open with almost clinical precision.

Her stomach looked shrunken, caved in and hollowed, the skin hanging limp and loose and ragged at her sides.

Her face, that was the hardest thing. One could stare at the viscera and pretend to be detached. Divorce your mind from the knowledge that this had been a living human being. But her face was untouched, but for a few splatters of blood. And that made it the worst thing of all, because he couldn't look at that face and pretend it was anything but a person.

The eyes were bulging, staring down at herself in bizarre fascination. The mouth rigid in a permanent scream. The lines of her face were frozen, distended. She seemed shocked by what she'd done to her own body. Terrified, horrified.

Rigor mortis, the Officer told himself.

Abruptly, he realized that the blood was clotted at the edges. That John's footsteps had smeared it after it had already begun to thicken.

That suggested that John had only found the body, rather than....

John had found her like this, had walked through the blood, then away. He'd gone back to the living room, sat in the easy chair, turned on the television, and started reading his book. He'd called the police. And then he'd just sat there for the last hour, almost catatonic.

His gorge rising, he crossed over, conscious of his footsteps squishing over the blood. The greasy slippery wet feel of it under his shoes.

He touched her.

Cold.

How long ago had the call been? An hour?

A body wouldn't get this cold in an hour.

Not unless John had done it earlier, and waited.

He turned around carefully. That was when he saw it.

There was a big red streaked smear against the corner of the refrigerator, up near the top. A speckled blood pattern decorated the adjoining wall.

He stared for a moment, breathing shallowly, as if trying to breathe in as little of the air of the room as possible.

Stepping carefully, he didn't want to slip in this blood, he didn't want to fall into it, he walked over to the refrigerator. He touched it. Almost fresh.

It had its own particular smell. Sweeter, not quite so rancid as the rest.

He stared at the adjacent surface of the refrigerator

There was a crumpled shape at the base of the refrigerator.

The Officer stared.

It was a tiny body, exquisitely detailed. Fingers, toes, arms, legs. It lay in its own tiny pool of blood. The top of its head was gone, smashed open, caved in. A tiny perfect face stared blankly, ending abruptly just above the eyes.

He ran. Unmindful of the slick clotting blood underfoot, he raced to get out of the room.

The Officer was back in the living room. It was quiet, except for his own breathing. The television was still muted as he'd left it. John was still sitting in his chair.

How long had he been in there?

A few seconds.

He thought back to the footsteps in the blood, the smears, as if from a tiny squirming body. The footsteps near the body, someone had knelt there. The tiny body, across the room, as if thrown. The Officer measured positions in his mind, trajectories.

The Officer took a minute to control himself. Then he walked over to John.

"She was pregnant," he said flatly.

John nodded. "We found out after the accident. She'd been pregnant. It seemed ironic. Allison's life had been taken away, and we'd been given this new one in exchange. There was a sense of God's balance there."

"The Doctors wanted to terminate. A paralyzed woman having a baby? Too risky. Allison wouldn't let them. It would be her only one. She'd never be able to have another, not in her condition. She was very strong willed, very determined. She'd always been that way."

He pulled some cards from his pocket and sat down.

"John?" he asked, "did you kill Allison?"

"Yes," John whispered. "No."

"John?" he asked, "may I use the phone?"

John nodded. The Officer called in and reported a double homicide, or a possible homicide/suicide.

"They'll be here soon," he told John, setting the phone down.

John nodded.

The Officer stared at his card, the neat printing dark on still crisp white cardstock.

"John," he said, "pay attention. I am arresting you on suspicion of murder. You have the right to remain silent, anything you say or do may be recorded and used in evidence against you. You have the right to legal counsel. If you have no lawyer or are unable to obtain a lawyer, we will contact legal aid for you. Do you wish to talk to a lawyer right now?"

John shook his head.

"Do you want to talk to a lawyer, John? You have to say yes or no."

"No."

He put his card away.

"Do you want to talk about it, John?"

Surprisingly, John nodded.

"Do you think that there's any plan to things? Or is it just pointless? Is there a God?"

"I don't know, John," the Officer said.

"We used to believe," John said. "We used to believe in Him, but now I don't know if I want to. I think I'd prefer it if it was just stupid unplanned things happening for no reason.

"It was a miracle you see. God doesn't need big, flashy miracles. He makes little ones. He shows his faith in us, the way we have faith in him.

"Allison was always the strong one. The determined one. She picked this apartment, did you know that?

"I don't think it's easy on anyone. Paralysis. It's got to be awful, one minute to be walking around, doing things, and then suddenly you're in a chair, and things like breathing or opening a book are achievements.

"We can't understand. I'd try to tell her, but she'd tell me I couldn't possibly understand. Her life, her body had meant so much to her. The power to simply do things..."

"Did I tell you she ran the Boston marathon two years ago? Or was it three?"

"Suddenly, she was in a chair. For no reason at all. A stupid trip around to the corner store and it was all over. There she was in a chair, and I had to turn her over regularly so she wouldn't get bedsores, and change her bedpan and hook her up to catheters. Her legs were just dumb inert sticks.

"It could have been worse, I guess. She could breathe on her own, and she had some limited motor control over her arms. A vertebra or two down and she'd have had more. A little farther up and she'd have had nothing.

"But the little she had left just made it that much more unbearable.

"Allison rejected it. The night we brought her home, I laid beside her, and she whispered in my ear, promising that she would walk again.

"She couldn't accept it. We'd both spoken to the Doctors. I knew there wasn't any hope. I mean, when the spinal cord is damaged it's damaged. It doesn't get better.

"We were offered counseling. To adjust to it. But she refused. She had decided. She was going to be normal again. She was going to take her life back.

"Sometimes I'd watch her, staring down, beads of sweat on her forehead, her eyes fierce and burning. Willing the senseless clay below her waist to move. To feel.

"Sometimes she would just cry.

"She'd get really angry. Angry with me, or just angry with life. When her nose got rubbed in it. When she couldn't reach the television remote control because it was on the table and she couldn't lift her arm that high anymore. Or even when she had it, but she couldn't make her fingers work the buttons.

"I tried to help, sometimes, and that just made her angry too. It was as if she felt that in trying to help her with her condition, I somehow perpetuated it.

"She seethed all the time, a cauldron of black emotions. She knew it but she couldn't control it. We never knew what would come boiling out or when. Anything could set her off.

"It must have been hell," the Officer said, flatly and with no sympathy. The stench of blood was thick in his nostrils.

"Then one day, her knee moved."

There Are No Doors in Dark Places – Page 104

"It was in March. Her breasts were swollen and round, and she was just starting to show. Her arms and legs had deteriorated, the muscle tone fading to jelly, the bones become thin. Round body, puny arms and legs, she joked that she was turning into Humpty Dumpty. An egg with a face painted on it. I didn't like those jokes, the way she said it, you could peel back a layer of cheer, like a scum on the surface of a can of paint, and you'd find this deep well of bitterness.

"I think she was beginning to regret the pregnancy.

"I imagine it happens to a lot of women at some point in their pregnancy. The feeling that it isn't your body anymore. That you've been hijacked by this thing growing inside you.

"It must be awful for a normal woman, but Allison had already lost so much of her body already...

"We were watching television, her chair was absolutely stationary and her right knee moved."

"We both saw it. My heart leaped, you know, as if something had jumped out of closet at me. We stared at each other, astonished. I think that by that time, she'd begun to give up.

"But her knee had moved. Allison stared at it, concentrated, and after a few minutes, we saw it tremble again.

"The Doctor's had told us it couldn't possibly happen. But it had.

"Allison began to get feelings. Or the ghosts of feelings. Sensations of place or pressure. You know how you can tell exactly where your arm is, even with your eyes closed? Things like that.

"We saw the Doctors. They diagnosed phantom sensations. Intense wish fulfilment. They recommended counseling. We stopped seeing the Doctors. Allison refused.

"This was her miracle, you see. She wasn't going to let anyone crush it.

There Are No Doors in Dark Places – Page 105

"She was getting it back.

"Not all at once. I mean, her arms and legs had deteriorated. She couldn't just get out of the chair and walk. Muscle goes incredibly fast when you're not using it. But, in little bits and pieces, it was coming back.

"We talked about it at night, lying in bed together. I would touch her. She'd say if she could feel it. I'd use ice cubes and rose petals, always finishing by rubbing it against her cheeks.

"It wasn't full sensation. It was dull and muffled, sometimes strong, sometimes weak. Sometimes so hardly there so she'd be afraid it had gone away completely and burst into tears.

"We promised ourselves that it would be enough. We bargained with God. We didn't need everything. So long as she got something back. Something more than being a thing in a chair, we'd be happy.

"I'd lay there, with my hand on her thigh. Firm thick flesh, now sagging and soft. Her willing the muscle to flex.

"Sometimes it did. Sometimes it would flex and she wouldn't know. I would tell her. Sometimes she could feel and not move; sometimes she'd move and not feel.

"The pregnancy continued. Allison read an article in Readers Digest about fetal tissue being used to help Alzheimer's and Parkinson's patients. You know? The ones with nerve deterioration? Stem cell research?

"She got the idea that, I don't know, the pregnancy was helping her body regenerate. All those fetal chemicals, causing new tissue to develop, some of it was affecting her. Women's bodies change with pregnancy.

"At first, we were elated. You know. It made so much sense. And it wasn't like a quadriplegic or para had ever gotten pregnant. Doesn't happen. We were unique. We thought we'd discovered....I don't know, something like the fountain of youth. Or recuperation. Nerve regeneration or something. Something that would make a big difference in a lot of lives. We joked about the Nobel Prize.

"But there was this bitter little kernel of fear in Allison.

"She never said it out loud, but it came in hints. It was this: What if it passes? All those slowly building irregular erratic sensations, the twitching the flexing. What if it all just stops and goes away and she would be trapped again?

"If it was the pregnancy that was making it happen? What would happen after the pregnancy?

"Would it all just go away? Stop? Would her child crawl out her womb and walk away with her life?

"Allison's moods returned, blacker than ever. She was afraid and angry.

"More and more of her body came back. Her toes wriggled easily now, and with me helping, she could almost stand in her chair. It was still erratic, like trying to find a station on an old radio, fading in and out, drifting into static. It frustrated her, that it was inconsistent. That it faded in and out. That she couldn't control it better.

"She told me once, that it was like a radio, and someone else was playing with the dial.

"I didn't say anything to that. I should have.

"She would have amazed the Doctors, if she'd been willing to see any of them. To let any see her.

"Sometimes her legs would move on their own. Sometimes, the sensations would fade in strongly, a moment of clarity on the radio. There were times when she slept, that I watched her legs kick feebly, hands clenching and unclenching, keeping time with her toes.

"By now, we could feel the baby. We could feel it kicking in the womb.

"Allison began to focus on the baby, her fears becoming deeper and darker.

"She began to talk as if it was the baby that was making her body move. That perhaps all pregnant women had that, baby signals, she called it, but that most women, women who controlled their bodies, simply overrode the signals and never noticed it. You'd only notice baby signals if there was nothing to override it. Like walking into an empty house.

"Every phantom twitch, every flux in sensation began to make her more paranoid, more moody. She'd panic if her leg suddenly moved and she hadn't willed it.

"She became resentful, feeling now, more than ever, a passenger in her own body.

"It wasn't always that way. She'd set herself a goal of walking again, and we worked towards it. We did exercises and movements in bed, practicing. I'd place her feet against my chest and let her push. Sometimes, she was almost happy. Almost like the old days.

"And sometimes she'd be sitting there, and her knee would start to bob, and her face would contort and her fists clenched as she willed it to stop, to do what she wanted it to.

"She began to hate the baby. To hate the pregnancy. At first, she joked about it. But the jokes became steadily more bitter until there was nothing funny about them at all.

"She no longer called it the baby. She called it "it," or "the invader," or "the parasite."

"It had taken over her body, it was using her, it was an "other." A stranger. Another person.

"The emotional rollercoaster became more intense. Black depressions. Screaming rages. Anguished wailing.

"She tried not to feel this way. On some rational part of herself, she would admit that there was no place for her resentment.

"But sometimes she couldn't help it.

"And at night, when she slept, I watched her arms and legs kick and twist, hands clenching and unclenching.

"She didn't want the pregnancy to end, fearing what might wait there. She wanted it to be over now. Her body grew ripe and swollen, breasts heavy with milk. Her arms and legs were still like pipe stems.

"She talked as if she and the baby were struggling for the body, and she was losing.

"The pregnancy was becoming difficult. She was bloated now. The baby kicked almost constantly.

"I tried to engage her. To follow her into her logic and lead her out. How could the baby have any wants or desires? It was safe in the womb; it had no experiences, no sight, no sound, no touch. There was nothing. Where could it get personality? Or motive? It was just a blank slate, waiting to be born.

"She talked about abortion in moments of black depression. It was much too late for that, of course, but still she talked about it. She hinted darkly at suicide. At ending both their lives.

"I decided to hide the sharp knives.

"I came home, around five o'clock. The smell hit me as soon as I opened the door. My heart pounded. I was so afraid something had happened. She'd miscarried, or did something crazy to get rid of the baby. I ran into the kitchen.

His hands squeezed the book.

"There she was.... I can't tell you how long I stood there, just looking, staring. I couldn't tear my eyes away from her face... That expression...."

"Yes," the Officer said.

"The expression was the worst part of it. The blood and the smell, the....body, it all lead toward that expression."

"I thought, 'How could she do this to herself? How could a human being do something like that?'"

"I was stunned. I was numb. I felt like a cow in a slaughterhouse. I'd stepped into the room and this great big hammer hit dead center and my mind wouldn't function. Little fragments of thought drifted around, not really connecting enough to make anything coherent.

"I remember thinking that someone should close her eyes. I had this image that dead people should look like they do in funeral homes. With make-up and their best clothes."

"I can't remember when I noticed the crying."

"It wasn't very loud, I guess. Or maybe I was too shocked. It just sort of seeped into my consciousness."

"It sort of pulled me away. Broke the spell of that awful expression."

"It was a baby, right there in the middle of the pool of blood. Sort of squirming weakly. It was alive."

"And I thought to myself, 'It's a miracle.'"

"I stepped into the pool of blood for it. I can't tell you what that's like: To step into this pool of rancid aging blood. To know that your wife's life was squishing wet and thick under your feet.

"I slipped a little. The thought of falling into it made me want to vomit, I almost did, I felt a thick greasy mass sliding up my throat. I swallowed hard.

"I reached down and I picked her up.

"The baby. Our baby.

"I cradled her in my arms. She wasn't really a good looking baby. She looked kind of thin and bony. We'd read enough books to know that was how newborns looked. That rosy fat cheeked look comes a little later.

"Blood stained my shirt, but it wasn't the baby's blood. I was thankful for that. Thankful that it had survived the hour or so that it had been there, waiting for me to come home.

"It looked up at me. Its eyes were focused.

"That's rare, you know. In babies. Rare, but not unheard of.

"Then, very clearly, very calmly, it said my name.

"It spoke with Allison's voice."

The Officer didn't hear his next words. He didn't need to.

With an instant of crystal epiphany, the Officer perfectly understood the expression on the dead woman's face.

The End

Neck Row Man Sea

Laurie was watching television late at night the first time the bad word drifted through her mind as casually as a cloud passing across a moonlit sky. Charlie was finally asleep in his crib. He'd been crying and irritable all night.

Laurie was exhausted and half dozing.

"Neck row man sea," she spoke aloud, meticulously pronouncing each syllable.

On her lap the black cat shifted, disturbed by the slight movement of her speech. It looked up at her and meowed. She looked down at its mismatched eyes, one blue, one green, and tousled its head.

Where had that come from? Laurie wondered.

Necromancy. That was black magic, wasn't it? She thought to herself.

She shrugged, she'd probably gotten it from the TV set as she was drowsing. She pushed the cat off her lap and looked at the clock: 3:00 AM it blinked.

It was time to go to bed. Mister Hunter the Caretaker would be by tomorrow to collect her part of the rent. He liked to come early, trying to catch her in her bathrobe so he could stare down her front.

It wasn't, she told herself, as if it was much of an apartment. She lived in a one bedroom apartment in an old drafty building. Charlie, her baby, occupied the bedroom, Laurie unfolded the couch in the living room.

Laurie hated being poor. Hated being alone and unwanted and slowly growing older as her child grew up. She hugged Sam, her cat, to her as she went to sleep.

She woke to a persistent knocking at her door.

"Oh damn," she mumbled, she stumbled over to the peephole.

It was Mister Hunter.

"Just a minute," she told him.

Laurie scrambled into her bathrobe before letting him in.

"Hey Laurie, I hope I didn't wake you," he said.

The way his eyes slid over her made her body feel like it had been dipped in oil. Mister Hunter was a greasy hairy man with a potbelly and pale rancid skin on the wrong side of forty. He always smelled vaguely of something she couldn't identify, something sour. He had a wife who was just as unpleasant, but that didn't stop him from hitting on the tenants.

"Uh, no," she said, "I was just putting on some tea."

Involuntarily he licked his lips. She flinched at her choice of words. Saying 'putting on' probably made him think of 'taking off.'

"I've got the money right around here," she told him, stepping into the kitchen area.

Welfare theoretically paid the rent, but it wasn't enough. So each month she gave the landlord forty dollars of the money welfare provided to her for food and clothing. Then, left short, she tried to figure out how to make it to the end of the month, so the cycle could start over again.

"That's okay," he told her, "I'm in no hurry."

He followed her into the kitchen and sat down at the little table.

"So," he asked, "what are you up to, these days?"

"Nothing much," she said, "taking care of the baby, looking for work."

She took the spending money out of a jar in cupboard and set it on the table. It jingled with the sound of nickels and dimes.

"Those two don't go together," he grunted, "you should get yourself a man."

Her bathrobe slipped a little and she could almost feel the pressure of his piggy little eyes on her exposed flesh.

"I had a man," Laurie told him, "he broke my nose when I was six months pregnant."

Carefully she counted out thirty five dollars.

"Yeah," he said, "that's tough. But still, I bet you must get pretty lonely all by yourself. I bet you'd like some 'company' once in a while." Hunter put a vaguely obscene lilt into the word 'company.' He folded the money away. It was mostly in ones and two's.

"I'm okay," Laurie replied stiffly, "I got Charley, and I got Sam."

"It's illegal to keep a pet in this building," Hunter told her. He laid his hand across her wrist. Her skin shriveled. "You're lucky I like you. Sometimes I wonder why I go out of my way for people."

Charley's bawling saved her from having to answer. Hunter flinched visibly at the sound.

"He probably just needs changing," she told him. There was a small pleasure in watching him squirm in disgust.

"I'd better be going, then. Let you take care of the kid."

He got up.

"Okay," she said, walking quickly into the bedroom.

Laurie picked up Charley and then stepped back to the hall.

"Wait..." she called to Hunter in the Doorway.

He turned.

"D'you know what 'necromancy' means?" she asked.

His greasy brow wrinkled.

"That's black magic shit. Workin' with zombies and dead things and stuff."

"I was just wondering," she told him.

"Uh huh," he said, "where'd you hear that?"

"On the TV last night."

"Oh," he announced dumbly, "I don't remember seeing no horror movies in the TV guide, I would have stayed up for it."

"I can't remember what show it was."

He gave her a broken toothed grin, "Oh well. You wanna stay up some night practicing black magic, that's fine with me. I'd even let you cast a spell on me."

The grin turned into a leer just before he vanished out the door.

Pig, she thought, as she held the baby.

Their conversation flitted through her mind as she changed the diaper. Looking for work: What a joke. Who was going to hire a nineteen year old high school dropout.

"You messed yourself, eh? Smells bad." She talked to Charley just to hear a human voice. "Better learn soon, I don't want to be changing your diapers for the rest of my life."

And if she could find a job, what would she do about Charley? Day care cost money. She couldn't earn enough to pay nursery fees and then rent and food and clothing on top of that.

Sam, her cat, meowed insistently, rubbing against her leg.

"Wait a minute, Sam," she muttered. Charley was still crying. Holding the baby in one arm she rocked it back and forth, carrying the diaper to a hamper in the bathroom, next to the litter box.

Sam followed her with cat quick steps. He meowed again.

"Wait, Sam..." Laurie shoved the cat with her foot, but it continued to follow her, "or I'll take you back to the pound."

Sam was what she thought of as her one luxury. She'd gotten him for free at the animal shelter. But he was her pick.

It was the week after Philip had broken her nose. She'd moved out, taking the television and two suitcases with her.

There was a bitter taste in remembering. What a slide that had been. High school had been a different world. They were going to graduate and then get married. They'd have jobs and a nice house. Philip had wanted a dog, but she'd always argued for a cat.

At least, she thought sourly, I have the cat. She opened the cupboard and pulled out the kitty kibbles.

The pregnancy had ruined everything. There had been the terrible fights with her parents as she'd tried to get an abortion, then moving in with Philip, the two of them dropping out of school as they'd tried to make it work.

She poured the kibbles into the bowl beside the garbage. A kibble or two bounced onto the linoleum.

"Eat up, you little monster," she told the cat.

But it hadn't worked. Philip had become increasingly withdrawn and bitter as the pregnancy progressed.

They'd even stopped making love. Except that Philip had never used that term. To Philip, it had always been fucking.

She'd tried. She'd been out there looking for a job too. And at home she'd done her best to make the rathole of an apartment a home. To make it neat and presentable. To always have a good meal on the table. Philip just got worse. More withdrawn, more resentful of her.

It was as if he was watching his future diminish as her belly grew.

As it turned out, she thought angrily, it was only her future that had been flushed down the toilet.

Walking back and forth across the kitchen with Charley, Laurie watched Sam wolf down the kibbles. She poured some water for him.

"What happened Sam?" she asked. "All I wanted was a life."

There Are No Doors in Dark Places – Page 117

The cat looked up and meowed.

She thought of a song. "Whatever happened to that ole black magic?"

The days drifted past in monotonous repetition. Charley demanded constant attention. When she wasn't changing him she was feeding him. When she wasn't feeding him she was rocking him. When she wasn't rocking him she was changing him. And so on, and so on, and so on. Right around the clock.

If it wasn't Charley, it was Sam: Demanding to be fed, demanding to be put outside, or simply demanding attention.

"I don't know why I got a cat like you," she would tell it.

"I ought to take you back and get a cat that'll mind its own business," she would threaten.

When she'd seen Sam at the animal shelter, a raggedy black tom with mismatched eyes, she'd felt a wave of sympathy for it. She'd still had a black eye at the time.

The shelter people told her that the cat had been there four weeks. They usually only kept them a week before putting them down, but they'd had it at a vet one week, and then they thought they might have found the old owner another week.

Things had come up, but it was all out of time.

If Laurie hadn't taken him home, they would have put Sam to sleep that very day.

In a way, she felt responsible for his life, just like Charley.

The cat would simply blink up at her when these thoughts crossed her mind.

Every now and then, in odd moments when Charley was quiet and Sam was purring on her lap, the word would bubble up to the surface of her thoughts. Like some log buried in a swamp, pushed to the top of the water by its own decomposition.

Or like a dead body rising through the muck.

Necromancy. Death magic. She was surprised at how much she knew once she started to think about it.

"Things just float in," she told Charley as she changed his diapers. "You watch movies and you hear TV. People talk. You pick things up without knowing."

"For instance, I know that you can't leave a baby alone with a cat. Did you know that?" she asked him as she turned him over and powdered his bum. Charley gurgled happily.

"It's because the cat will smell milk on the baby's breath, and he'll sit on the babies chest and try and lap it up, lap up the taste of milk on their breath, and the baby will suffocate from the weight. Now did either of you know that?"

Sam rubbed against her leg.

"Well, it's true. I don't know where I learned it from, but it's true. That's why I don't allow you in the bedroom, Sam." She directed her comment to the cat as she fixed the new diaper in place on Charley.

Necromancy, she realized, was death magic. It took its energy from the sacrifice of living things like chickens or goats. She'd seen them kill a chicken once on some television show about voodoo. Paid in blood up front.

Magic, the thoughts came to her, always had a price. You paid for it sooner or later.

Like loan sharks, she thought, the longer you waited the more it cost.

One morning, at the end of the week, she opened the fridge and was assaulted by the rank odor of spoiled milk and rotting food.

"Fridge's busted," Hunter grunted, when he finally came down to inspect it.

"All my food is ruined," Laurie wailed miserably. The tone in her voice made Sam meow questioningly. It was a week and a half before the next welfare cheque.

"Nothing I can do but get someone in to fix it. Take a few days to get someone in to fix it, maybe a week," Hunter said.

"I have a baby," Laurie whined, "I need a fridge."

"I'm sorry about that..." Hunter began.

"Please," she begged.

A look passed across his face, "I might be able to do something, but you'll owe me..."

Later that night she sat in the kitchen, holding Sam in her arms, watching the mini-fridge chug away in the corner. She'd borrowed twenty-five dollars for food. There would be a price, she knew.

Laurie was shocked by how much this relatively trivial disaster had affected her.

Back in high school, before everything went wrong, she wouldn't have cared. She'd have just gone to MacDonalds, or eaten at friends.

Except that now there was no money for MacDonalds, and none of her old friends were around, they'd dropped her when their lives had gone one way and hers had gone another. To them, she was an ugly might-have-been that they'd managed to avoid and didn't want to be reminded of.

No new friends had replaced them. You couldn't go out and meet people when you were looking after a kid twenty-four hours a day.

What hurt the most was that Philip had never looked for her, had never called, after she walked out.

Poverty sucked, she decided. Being poor meant you had no chances. You couldn't have good toys for Charley; or medicine if he got sick. You couldn't afford a babysitter. You couldn't go out. You couldn't do anything. The high point of the week became taking Charley out for a walk, if the weather was good. All you could really do was sit around and watch TV and get fat and old.

"I wish," she mumbled, "I wish for a way out."

But, she thought, there were no fairy godmothers to wave a magic wand. And anyway, if there were, they'd probably have a price. Like everything else.

Sam squirmed in her arms.

As she counted down the nights until welfare day, she thought about it again and again.

Necromancy was black magic, sure, but at least you paid up front and that was that. Once she turned her attention to it, it all seemed so straightforward. Even the rituals were just common sense.

In a way, it was like Birthday candles, she thought. Blowing out the candle and making a wish was a magical ritual. But with a candle, you were only making a tiny sacrifice.

Too bad it didn't work.

Still, on welfare day, she half-surprised herself by buying a rabbit at the Pet Store.

She'd thought about getting a chicken, like in the voodoo program. But the Pet Store didn't have live chickens and the meat market only had dead ones.

Besides, the idea of a chicken made the whole thing seem unbearable. How would she get it home without making noise? And what about the sacrifice, she'd shuddered at the memory of the headless chicken flopping around and beating its wings in the voodoo show.

A rabbit wouldn't make noise. Besides, she thought, if she changed her mind, she could keep it as a pet.

Laurie kept the rabbit for two days. At first, feeling its soft fur and looking at its sensitive twitching nose and soft brown eyes she didn't have the heart to hurt it. Sam sniffed it once or twice and then ignored it.

It shit on the rug and gnawed at the electrical cords.

Unlike Sam, it seemed to have no personality, it just hopped around. The rabbit didn't seem to like her, she had to chase it to pet it. Then it hopped away as soon as she released her grip, moving until it was just out of her reach, and then snuffling about, indifferent to her presence.

At night, Laurie could hear it moving around, scrabbling like some huge rat. It made it hard for her to sleep; she thought it kept Charley awake too.

"You could do it," the thoughts floated through her mind, "in the bathtub. That way, the blood could just drain away." The bathroom was all tiles: Easy to clean, quiet, no windows, no one could hear.

She lay on her back in bed and listened to its scratching and thought about it. Reaching up, she scratched Sam, who was laying on her stomach, behind the ears.

"What about it Sam?" she asked, "Do you want to be a witch's familiar?"

Sam just blinked his eyes a couple of times and purred.

The next night, at midnight, she took the rabbit into the bathroom.

It was harder than she thought it would be. She had to hold the rabbit with both hands as it kicked. The incantations came out as a mumbled hiss. Blood spattered on the walls and across her face.

Afterwards, she simply felt stupid.

Laurie couldn't sleep. She laid in bed until the morning, conscious of an eviscerated rabbit tucked into the miniature fridge's vegetable compartment. She became aware of Sam lapping traces of dried blood from her skin and pushed him off the bed.

The next morning, she was bone tired. Charley seemed more bothersome than usual. Neither feeding nor changing helped, he complained continually.

"Be quiet," she told Charley as she walked him back and forth, "your mommy is going crazy. Cabin fever. That's what it is, being cooped up here with you two all the time."

"Isn't that right, Sam?" she asked.

Sam was eating pieces of rabbit meat in his bowl. The cat didn't even look up.

Two days later, while taking Charley for a walk she found an unmarked envelope containing four hundred dollars in cash.

Back in her apartment she put Charley away, and sat at the kitchen table, counting the money over and over again. Sam's meowing went unheard. It was more than she got from welfare. Her mind became a swirling flood of all the things she could buy, toys for Charley, clothes, food, she could get a babysitter, go to a movie.

At the back of her mind, though, was the idea that the magic had worked, after all. There was a strangely satisfying feeling that came with that thought. It meant that it wasn't just luck, it had been her. She'd supported her family; she'd done something.

The money lasted a week. A glorious week of potato chips and ice cream, eating at MacDonalds. A week of catnip and educational toys and that special quality baby powder that Charley really seemed to like. A week of baby clothes and new jeans that made her feel sexy and attractive for the first time in a year. A wonderful week that brought home to her how bland and stale her life had been.

And would be again.

She bought a guinea pig, the biggest one the store had. This time, she didn't let the little rodent shit all over the apartment for two days. She did it that night.

The next day, while cleaning Charley, she picked up the phone and answered a radio quiz. She won a Blu-Ray and six months digital streaming service.

"It's working," she crooned to Charley during feeding, "it's finally working out. We're going to have a good life.

We're going to be a terrific family, the three of us, wait and see."

She did the laundry, did everything that could be put in a washer, even dishtowels, using that expensive fabric softener that made things smell so good. She scrubbed the linoleum floor in the kitchen and polished the counters and coffee tables. The apartment was still a low rent dive, she admitted, but now it felt brighter and more hopeful. Now it seemed like a home. Even

Mister Hunter was bearable, actually pleasant at times.

A form casually filled out won her the Children's Universal Encyclopedia Set. There were more rabbits and guinea pigs, and rats and puppies and half grown dogs, some chickens, and even a young goat.

Even Charley seemed more pleasant. The fussy irritation that had made him so difficult the last few months vanished. Now he was a happy, gurgling baby. Feeding and changing him were no longer chores, perhaps it was simply that there was more to look forward to. She spent hours playing with him.

It was neat at first. Laurie never knew what form things would take. There was a fifty dollar rebate on her electric bill. Then she found a diamond ring inside a coat she bought from at the Goodwill Seconds store. At times, it became almost irritating, she didn't often get what she really needed when she needed it. A free prescription had come only after devastating menstrual cramps had passed.

"If you were a better familiar," she scolded Sam, shaking the prescription at him, "these things would come in on time."

She'd begun to think of Sam as a real familiar. That was why he'd lasted four weeks at the shelter. Sam, she thought, was feeding her magical knowledge, just putting it in her head.

After a time, it occurred to her that it was still just the three of them, a lonely little circle.

Laurie returned to her old haunts to find that many of her friends had moved on. The gulf between her and the ones she found convinced her that there was nothing left in the past.

She tracked down Phillip's phone number. For a quarter of an hour she sat by the phone, desperately holding Sam like a rag doll. Finally, with muffled sobs, she tore up the piece of paper with the phone number and flushed the bits down the toilet.

At midnight, embarrassed by the fact of her nudity, Laurie stepped into the bathtub with the sacrifice for the first time. I need someone, she thought. Holding the rabbit above her head, she slit it's throat. It kicked spastically as hot blood spurted on her cheek and ran down her neck, dripping redly over her breasts and thighs.

It was like birthday candles, you just made your wish and blew them out.

Three days later the serviceman came from the cable company because she'd won a year's free cable service in a draw at the Safeway.

He was gorgeous. She'd made him tea and then they'd talked for most of the morning. His hand on her thigh, when it came, was welcome and she opened easily.

He was better than Philip. Much, much better than Philip, and it had been so long. His name was Mike, and he promised that he would come back.

After he left, she just laid there on the bed, languorous and sensual in her wet nudity. Padding onto her stomach, crouching at her sternum, the cat licked the drying sweat from between her breasts.

The next day, Laurie was still glowing. Singing softly to herself she straightened up the apartment, Sam following her, meowing softly for attention.

Mike had left his newspaper behind, in the kitchen.

Laurie hardly ever bought newspapers. Except for the comics, there wasn't much in them that interested her.

Late that night, as she read the newspaper, she came across the National lottery listings. The National lottery was held once a week, the prize was nominally a quarter of a million dollars. But if there was no winner, then the prize would roll into next week's lottery, and so on, until someone won the pot. It was up to four million dollars.

Laurie thought vaguely that it would be nice to win something big for a change. Then she turned to the comics. After that, she tried to do the crossword puzzle.

Over the next week, the thought of the lottery would intrude upon her at odd moments. When changing Charley she would daydream about winning the lottery and having a housekeeper to do this.

Four million dollars, she thought, would solve all her problems.

Finally, she bought a ticket and the day before the draw, she sacrificed a rabbit. She'd become quite elaborate in her sacrifices, buying a red satin nightgown to wear, now bloodstained, chanting for as much as half an hour, and killing with a genuine silver plated knife she purchased specially for the purpose at Walmart.

She lost. The prize went unclaimed.

"Magic," she told Sam, "is damned frustrating."

The cat just blinked at her with mismatched eyes.

Still, the smaller magics seemed to work. New things happened. She cleaned the apartment, played with Charley, rented movies and watched TV. Mike phoned to tell her he would be going out of town for a week, but would call her when he got back.

The next week, she bought a ticket and tried again.

Again the lottery went unclaimed.

Five and a half million dollars now.

The sacrifice wasn't big enough, she decided.

Laurie bought a goat.

She'd used a goat once before and had promised herself never again. The beast had kicked and butted and made noise. It had been murder getting it home unseen, and once home, it had nearly wrecked the bathroom before it had been time. She'd been terrified by the possibility that it might wake the neighbors. Afterwards she'd had to laboriously cut it to pieces and spent half the night disposing of the carcass as far across the city as she could walk.

This goat, an obnoxious black Billy, was an even bigger pain in the ass.

Again, the prize slipped away from her.

Six and three quarter million dollars.

Failure put her in a black mood. For two days, she moped.

It's too big, the thought slipped into her mind, it's not like some supermarket draw or radio contest. Millions of people buy tickets. What was needed was a really big sacrifice.

She petted Sam, he preened under her hand. Animals just wouldn't release enough death energy. She needed a more powerful sacrifice.

A human sacrifice.

In the bedroom, Charley cried.

She stood there a moment, allowing the pieces to fall into place in her mind.

Her response was simple.

"No," she said out loud. She went to take care of Charley.

Seven million dollars. Unclaimed.

As the next week passed, Laurie found she couldn't stop thinking about it. It began to obsess her. Seven million dollars she would chant unconsciously as she changed diapers or cleaned the toilet.

Seven and a quarter million.

On Wednesday at 4:25 p.m., she broke.

Laurie threw the kibbles box at Sam. With a puzzled "Rrowl!" the cat leaped away.

"This is all your fault," she screamed at the cat.

"You're doing it. You put the magic in my head. You're making me think this."

In the next room, startled by the noise, Charley started to cry.

"I don't need you," she blubbered as she chased the cat around the apartment, "I don't need that money. I can do the magic by myself now, I know how."

She caught Sam by the scruff of his neck. Holding the struggling animal at arm's length, Laurie marched it out of the building. It howled as she flung it away.

The cat hit the ground, bounced, and scrambled away.

"I don't need you," she said bitterly.

Seven and a half million.

The magic stopped working. She made sacrifices practically every night, but nothing happened except that she ran increasingly short of money.

Charley began to cry constantly. It kept her up at nights. The Doctor said it was just teething, and would be over in a few months.

Seven and three quarter million.

Laurie had reconciled herself to the knowledge that Mike wasn't going to call. On the other hand, Mister Hunter had become unpleasantly aggressive. His wife was in the hospital. Some of his advances contained veiled threats.

She fantasized about making Mister Hunter a sacrifice. But she remembered the goat with a shudder, if the goat had been bad, Hunter would be a hundred times worse. Besides, deep down she felt that Hunter wouldn't satisfy the magic. She knew what it wanted.

Sometimes in the night, she heard Sam calling plaintively outside.

Bills came in the mail, but even worse were the flyers: Sign here and subscribe to the Children's book series. Buy the video clubs library membership, seven rentals a week for the price of five. Expand cable to the superchannels. New appliances. A car. A laptop. Clothes. Everyone wanted her to buy something, but she had nothing to pay them with.

Charley cried and fussed, and the apartment became grey and barren. She felt her life closing in around her again.

"It's just you and me kid," she told Charley as she rocked him.

He just cried. That was all he did nowadays, he never even wanted to play.

She felt increasingly stupid talking to him.

She found no trace of personality in him. More and more, he was just a bundle of chores.

Demanding feeding.

Demanding changing.

Just demanding.

Eight million dollars.

Late in the night, as Charley squalled and squalled, she finally let the cat in.

Much later, she was blearily conscious of weeks, even months, having passed.

Her lawyer was talking to her. She didn't especially care. She simply sat there in her hospital gown and let him drone on. The past was a blur.

No, that wasn't quite true, she remembered Philip, and Sam, and then Charley. Then she didn't want to remember any more. She didn't want to think about anything. She didn't want to be.

Laurie noticed a razor blade on the table between them. Had he put it there? Carefully, surreptitiously, she palmed it.

Tonight, she thought. One last bloodletting. A final sacrifice and then it, then she, would be over.

She looked up at her lawyer for the first time. He was a striking man, she thought through the mental haze, sharp features and dark hair. But his eyes were his most arresting feature: Mismatched, one blue, one green.

The End

Suicide Generation

"I did it," the Killer said. "Oh yes. I did it. Your wives, your daughters. I cut them open, I gutted them like trout. I wrapped their innards around me like wet feather boas, and danced in front of the biggest mirrors I could find."

He puffed on his cigar and looked up. He stared defiantly at the men who surrounded him.

"There ain't nothin' like the feel of human innards, all wet and steaming, wrapped around your naked body."

His nose wrinkled for a second.

"Can't say I care much for the smell though. That's why I took to cigars."

Constable James Donovan, the largest of the men gathered around, vomited.

* * *

"What's the story on this guy?" Carpenter asked.

The men were gathered around the table.

"We caught him in the act, or the husband did, anyway. He came home from work early one day, and he found this guy, standing in his living room, stark naked and covered in blood."

That was Donovan, the first responder on the murder scene. The forensic team was still out there. Picking up bits and pieces of mother and child with tweezers, trying to figure out which was which.

"He'd been working with the wife and daughter for about two hours, we figure. They were kind of scattered around."

Donovan's partner, Rosario.

"The husband turned around and just started screaming. Seems, Kelsey had a gun. He got the poor bastard halfway down the lawn," Donovan said.

"Shot a couple of neighbors, drove away in the station wagon."

"He hadn't cleaned himself up though. Hands were slippery. He got about four blocks when he lost control, wrapped it around a pole. That's where we nailed him. He just surrendered to me."

This was from the youngest in the group, Levett. He looked like a traffic cop. Young and gangly, everything about him screamed punk.

The duty Sergeant cleared his throat. "We link him with at least four similar murders in the last year. Including the ones in your jurisdiction. That's why we put a special call in for you."

"Probably more than that," Carpenter said. "Fifteen or twenty, maybe. These guys don't start off this twisted. Usually they work up to it. We'll have to search a lot of jurisdictions files, see where he's been."

"We haven't done the interview yet, we were waiting for you," the Sergeant said.

"We cleaned him up though," Donovan offered. He looked a little green around the gills.

"Any advice on talking with this guy," Kelsey asked.

"They lie to you, these shies. Sometimes they'll take the credit for everything in sight. Sometimes they'll lie just to be obstinate. They never admit to killing any place with a death penalty."

Carpenter paused.

"As far as they're concerned, they're all alone in the world. The rest of us don't matter."

* * *

"Why?"

There Are No Doors in Dark Places — Page 132

"Why?" the Killer laughed. "You boys asked Speck that? Or Manson? Or Bundy? Dahmer? Huberty? What did they tell you? I'll go with what they said. Don't matter. It's all bullshit."

"What's your reason?"

The Killer stared at him, suddenly sober.

"Why do you need to know?"

"Because I need to know."

Suddenly, the Killer seemed almost compassionate.

"You think I can give you an answer that'll help you stop someone else. That don't work son. Otherwise, all the answers those other guys give would make a difference."

"I want to understand, it will make a difference."

"You think understanding will help? That it will make it better, somehow, if you know why? It won't."

"Let me be the judge of that."

"Sometimes knowing makes it worse. Sometimes it's better not to know, cause once you do, you can't get rid of it. Just knowing can change a man."

* * *

"So who is this piece of shit?" Carpenter asked.

"Local guy," the Sergeant said. "Irregularly employed, drinks a bit. We've got a couple of drunk and disorderlies on him. But that's about it. Basically: He's nobody."

"Well," said Kelsey, "I guess he's somebody now."

"No," said Carpenter, "I won't give him that. He's not somebody, he isn't anybody. As far as I'm concerned, he's out of the human race."

"Just some big cockroach," Rosario said, "needing to be stepped on."

"Something like that," Carpenter said.

* * *

Finally, the Killer shrugged.

"The real reason, no bullshit, no excuses."

There was no answer. The only sound was the slow click of the tape recorder, turning.

The Killer laughed.

"Shit, Son! You're a real hard boy!"

"I guess I could tell you that my Pa beat me, but I heard tell of boys got beaten lots worse than me. Maybe I whacked off over too many Penthouse magazines at an impressionable age. Maybe it was the demon rum. Maybe it was just the devil."

He took another long hard drag.

"Maybe I just liked it. Maybe I just liked the feel of innards wrapped around my hardon."

He looked up at the man, staring through hooded eyes.

"Maybe you'd like the feel too? You never know."

Carpenter was silent.

The Killer coughed. He grinned at the men, before turning to Carpenter.

"You're a tough guy, all right."

"The truth," Carpenter whispered.

"All right then," the Killer said, "the truth."

"The truth, the real truth, it has nothing to do with what those guys said. Nothing to do with what's inside my head, or Gacy's. We're just the ones in the wrong place at the wrong time."

He expelled a long draught of smoke, carefully blowing three smoke rings.

"Ever hear of the suicide generation?"

They said nothing.

"My Pa was a dog breeder. Respectable trade. I used to help him put down the old dogs, the bad breeds. Maybe that was how I got started. What do you think?

"You might of heard, then again, you might not. A lot of inbreeding goes on with dogs. They don't much care.

There Are No Doors in Dark Places – Page 134

Breeders care though. Breeders start to notice that you inbreed a strain too much, and it starts to go bad.

"Dogs get all twitchy and nervous. Health is bad. Temper is bad. Breed too far, suddenly, you got an animal you can't do anything with. I figure everyone knows that.

"What only breeders know, what we heard, is that if you keep on going. Keep on inbreeding that strain, suddenly, it goes real bad. Suddenly, you got bitches eating their pups. Studs tearing up their dams, or going at each other.

He laughed softly.

"We don't have a name for it, when a bloodline goes rotten like that. We hear it's out there, and we got no intention of taking that road. What's the use of naming a place you ain't never planning on visiting?"

"It was scientists that put a name to it. You know, those guys breeding rats and mice and rabbits for their laboratory experiments. They liked inbreeding. The closer together their mice were, the more likely their experiments would be specific."

"Then they found the suicide generation. All you have to do is breed far enough and the line goes bad. The animals are crazy, mothers eat their babies, gangs rove looking for victims to tear apart, adults kill each other. It's like the whole line is committing suicide."

"I've heard about experiments with rats," Kelsey offered.

"Rats are the ones they like to use. To talk about social pressure, crowding or something causing things to break down. It ain't just rats. They found it with mice, with rabbits, even with cows. Anything you want to breed, it'll have a suicide generation.

"Even in the wild, they got it. You remember all those pictures of lemmings going over a cliff.

"It's like there's instructions written into the genes. We go past a certain point, and it's like it says to just turn it off. Shut down the whole race. Clean the house and start over, or let something else start over.

"We got it too. We're on the suicide generation. It starts with the weak. With guys like me and Dahmer. But everyone feels it, it spreads. It's game over man."

"I don't see us as all that inbred," Carpenter whispered.

"Yeah, I think we're past due. We've been putting it off for a long time now.

"The world is full of empty cities. Ruins. Nobody knows what happened. One day, it was just full of people. Then it's all gone. Their turn came. I figure it's been happening off and on for a long time, whenever places close in. "

A thought seemed to strike him.

"Maybe longer than anyone can remember," he laughed suddenly. "Anybody seen a Neanderthal man lately? I heard they was doing pretty good for a while there?"

He sobered.

"I think we're way past due. I think we've been putting it off for a long time, and now it's closing in on us. It's the suicide generation, this one or the next. But it's right on top of us."

"I figure the black plague might have helped. You know, set the clock back for a bit. Then there was Columbus and those guys. Always going new places, always finding new things. All those discoveries and inventions like airplanes and TV. I bet that put it off, slowed it down a lot. Took some steam off."

"Maybe even internet for a while, but I think that's starting to make it worse."

"But now...now we've been to the moon. We've been every place there is to go. We got nowhere left to run to hide from ourselves. No more tricks to pull out of the hat.

"We've had a good long run. We've put it off for the longest time. Though maybe we were just spreading the poison farther, making it take more time to build up a proper head.

"Before, it was just cities someplace, and everywhere else, life went on.

"This time..."

He let the thought hang.

"Everyone's cruel now, have you noticed? The right, the left, police, politicians. There's no kindness any more, just cruelty. Priests... Presidents."

The cigar was almost finished. He inspected it critically between his fingers, and then stubbed it out on the desk, ignoring the ashtray before him.

"Can I have another one?" he asked mildly.

"So it's not you at all, is it?" The Sergeant asked. "Society's to blame."

The Killer laughed.

"Hello? Hello? Were you listening, boy? It is me, and everyone else. And society? Societies over. Society's fucked."

"You're fucked," Carpenter shouted, suddenly angry. "You're the one that's fucked. I'd shoot you myself right now, but I know that you aren't going to last a week in confinement. We're all going to dance on your grave."

"Tell me something, Son," the Killer said. "I'd really like to know."

"What?" asked Carpenter, shocked at his own outburst. He shoved the anger down. Professional, he thought, I'm a professional.

"Did it help? Did it make things better to know what it is? Are you feeling better, now that you're told that a big black thing is bearing down on you and there's nothing you can do? Is this kind of knowledge really better than ignorance?"

Carpenter stared for a long moment.

"Go to hell," he said quietly.

The Killer started laughing as the man stalked away.

"I don't need to go anywhere, boy. It's coming to us."

* * *

The drive home was a two and a half hour commute. He was exhausted. For a brief moment he considered checking into a hotel room rather than take the drive. But his wife was waiting at home. He didn't like to leave her alone.

Not with the crime rate the way it was.

He drove down the dilapidated streets, negotiating his way around the potholes. It was dark enough for streetlights now, but he noticed only every second or third was on.

They must have shot them out, he thought. Damned animals.

He drove past old buildings with boarded up windows. Newer ones looking bruised and battered, graffiti covering them like a cancer. There were bars and metal screens on all the windows.

There weren't many people out.

Where do they all go? He wondered.

He turned on the radio.

"...postpartum depression," blared for a moment until he turned the volume down. "...long recognized as a medical condition, health sciences have increasingly begun to re-evaluate its impact...." static as he passed some powerlines, "Studies show that the leading cause of death among inner city black infants is suffocation or strangling by their mothers."

A taped expert's voice cut in, "...this is a statistical anomaly produced by improved health care across the board. The infants most susceptible to this treatment were previously dying of other factors. If you look at historical charts, you can see that overall infant mortality rates have actually declined."

More static, then another expert. "...symptomatic of lack of social services available to inner city mothers, and of family breakdowns, leaving..."

There Are No Doors in Dark Places – Page 138

Abruptly, he shut off the radio. It reminded him too much of that mad conversation.

The world's always ending, he reminded himself, and it never does.

He stopped at a light. A car full of youths pulled up beside him. The boys stared coldly at him. Punks or punk wanna-bees, dressed in gangland outfits. Were they really a gang, or just painfully stupid kids, caught up in ugly fashion?

They stared. He stared back at them.

Come on, you little shits, he thought angrily. I'm tired of this. You think you can beat up little old ladies. You think you're tough. You aren't the only ones with guns. Try me, try me, you...

The one in the driver's seat leaned forward.

He reached for his gun.

The youth's car lurched forward. Startled, he realized that the light had turned green.

He took a deep breath, shocked again by his sudden anger.

How did things get so completely fucked up? He wondered.

He resumed driving.

* * *

The next morning he heard that the Killer was found strangled in his cell, hanging from his socks from the drainage pipe of the sink.

It was being ruled a suicide. Nobody was interested in looking too close.

When he heard, all he could think was "good."

It wasn't, he thought to himself, as if a human being had died.

When do they stop being human beings? He wondered.

When do they become things?

* * *

He pulled into the Seven-Eleven. It was late at night and he had a list with him.

Out here, all the streetlights worked. He wondered how much longer that would last, before the rot that infested the cities would seep out here.

Not long, he judged. Not by the looks of the wayward youths who hung around the seven eleven. They stared sullenly at him, bundled in their denim and flannels.

Don't they ever go home? He wondered. Or do they just hang here, like flies on rotten meat, doing sleazy little drug deals, fornicating in dumpsters, shooting up or maybe just shooting?

He had to shoulder his way past a callow young man. The boy had a pierced eyebrow and a stringy beard. He smelled of stale sweat.

He realized that he felt no human connection with them whatsoever. They might as well have been cockroaches. The aptness of the connection made him smile slightly.

The clerk inside wasn't much better. A pimpled collection of adolescent gangliness.

My god, he thought, was I ever that young? Or that ugly?

A couple of the kids from the parking lot came into the store. He glanced at them as he paid.

Here to do a little casual shoplifting? He thought.

The clerk bagged his items, made change and handed him the receipt.

He was half way out the store before he realized that the clerk had short changed him by two dollars.

"You little shit," he swore. The bag slipped from his fingers as he reached for his gun. He probably did it to everyone. Just a mistake, he'd say, if people caught on.

He wheeled and pumped seven rounds into the clerk. He watched as the boy jerked, gouts of blood kicking up from his body, falling back into the cigarette display.

The empty clip ejected automatically, he reached into his pocket for a fresh one. Always carry a spare, he thought.

The lot rats were frozen, inside and outside the store. He didn't have to look at them to know that their eyes were wide, mouths gaping.

Cockroaches.

Abruptly he realized that the store had security cameras. He'd been recorded. He was screwed. Screwed from the grave by that little turd behind the counter. Screwed by useless know-nothings who had no business being here in the first place.

Abruptly a snatch of words came through the muzak "Suicide Generation." That was where the ignorant slug had picked up the phrase for his bullshit explanation. It was just bullshit. It was all bullshit. Everything was bullshit.

It didn't help, he thought suddenly, it didn't help to know these things at all.

One clip left, he thought. Then he'd have to get some more. He'd have to act fast.

The cockroaches were just staring at him.

He turned to the next one and raised his gun.

The End

The Wizards of Huckleberry Finn

Franco watched the killer through the one way glass for exactly ten minutes. In that time he smoked three cigarettes, carefully shielding their glow with his hand. He tried to reconcile the savage mutilations he had reviewed, with this passive, almost catatonic, young man.

Finally, he stubbed out his last cigarette and entered the room. There was a subliminal whir as the video camera on the other side of the room recorded the interview.

"Jeff?" Franco prompted. The youth did not look up. He was twenty-five but looked eighteen, with a sallow complexion and corn blond hair that laid flat across his forehead as if wet with sweat.

"Jeff? I'm Doctor Franco; I'm here to assess you."

"You think I'm a sick bastard," Jeff mumbled without looking at him.

He's psychic, Franco thought sourly, and then started when Jeff nodded slightly.

"You are accused of, and have admitted to nine murders," Franco replied softly, "Particularly gruesome murders. That's all I know, that's all I'm going to know, unless you talk to me."

Jeff finally raised his head to look at him.

"It weren't nine murders. I killed one person, just nine times is all."

Franco let a pause slip by, watching for any action or reaction, carefully ticking off seconds. Jeff's stare shifted from apathetic to almost defiant.

Finally.

"Tell me how that can be," Franco asked.

Another five seconds ticked past before Jeff spoke.

"You believe in magic, Doctor?" he asked.

"Is that what you believe in?" Franco responded.

"Didn't figure that you would," Jeff laughed suddenly, "maybe you believe in psychic powers. A scientific man like you, sure you must believe in those."

Franco made a cradle of his fingers and rested his chin in them, he looked serious and sober.

"Go on," he said.

"I got them," Jeff told him, suddenly serious, "I got them real good. I can read people like books sometimes."

He laughed, "That's pretty good ain't it, seeing as how I can't read books themselves hardly at all. It's like there's all kinds of different gifts."

Franco felt that Jeff was drifting into grandiose fantasy, time to lead him back.

"You have powers," he agreed, "how did that lead you to kill those people? How did that lead you to kill Sara Ann Mobley?"

Jeff's grin faded slowly.

"I didn't kill Sara Ann Mobley."

That was correct as far as it went, Franco recalled sourly. Technically, he hadn't quite killed her. She had died in the hospital of bronchial hemorrhaging, a complication of her condition. He had in fact taken her to the hospital himself in a vain attempt to save her life. That was how the police had caught him.

He hadn't technically killed her: He had taken an innocent fourteen year old girl, and he had carefully broken her spine, inducing paralysis. Then he had methodically scooped out her eyeballs with a 'Victorian Edition' collectors tea spoon, pierced her eardrums with knitting needles, burned out her nose with ammonia, excised her tongue with a red hot Bowie knife and carefully seared the most sensitive areas of her skin, regardless of whether she could feel it or not, and she did feel some of it.

For reasons known only to himself; he had carefully sewn her navel and her vagina shut. Bound her arms and legs securely, even though, paralyzed as she was, she was certainly not going anywhere. At some point, he had even seen fit to deliberately break both her legs.

He had kept her alive in that unspeakable state for four months.

Jeff colored, as if he had tracked all of this through Franco's mind.

Franco felt the beginnings of harsh nausea.

"I killed Joshua LeBard." He put a harsh accent on the last name, making it sound like LEE-baR.

Franco wrote down the name.

"Who was he?" he asked softly.

"He was my best friend," Jeff replied, "but I had to kill him. They were all Joshua, so I had to do every one of them."

* * *

"See if you can find anything on a Joshua LeBard. Apparently born around the same time as the subject in the same general area. Died around age of fourteen. African-American with piebald coloration. Mother known as Hettie LeBard. Look for anything suspicious about his death," Franco suggested.

Lieutenant Martins jotted down the notes with crisp efficiency.

"Another possible homicide?"

"Who knows?" Franco answered, he kept trying to light his cigarette, but it wouldn't catch. Finally he threw it away.

"After all this, who cares?"

He stalked away.

"See you tomorrow, Doc," the Lieutenant called. Yes, Franco thought, tomorrow was the next appointment.

He hurried down the steps and out to his car. Only when he was driving did he begin to relax. He lit a cigarette.

He drove. He didn't feel like driving straight home, his wife was on a sabbatical. She wouldn't be back for another month, the house was too empty without her.

He simply drove, feeling safe and secure in plush comfort and steel frame, clear glass and horsepower giving him as much of the world as he wanted to deal with.

Franco found himself passing through the red light zone, smiling hookers with painted faces and out thrust breasts beckoned to his car.

Inside its shelter he blushed and scurried home.

* * *

"Joshua LeBard was born on the same day you were, just seven miles away from your hospital. Isn't that right?" Franco didn't even wait for Jeff's nod, he went on. "You went to the same integrated schools, lived in the same town."

Franco looked up from his notes.

"He drowned April 17, 1982."

"That's right," Jeff agreed softly.

"Death by misadventure, it says here," Franco said, "homicide ruled out. Hell, that's practically natural causes."

Jeff didn't say anything.

"Who was Joshua?" Franco asked. "And why did you have to keep killing him over and over."

Except you didn't kill him over and over. He drowned, apparently all by himself, and you went on to kill Tyler Ridgefield, and Elly Soames, and Wayne Washington, and

Myles Pirra, and Erma Louise Hampstead, and Sally Finlay, and Jerry Killian, and Dwight Elton, and Sara Ann Mobley.

He found he could recall the names of every victim.

Jeff looked drawn and tired, he took a deep breathe, seemed to gather strength within himself.

"Josh had the power too. I was born with the caul, you know what that is?" Jeff asked.

Franco nodded, it was part of the placental membrane, or the embryonic sack, that sometimes remained on baby's heads when they were born, almost like a cap. Old tales said it was a sign of supernatural gifts. Jeff continued.

"So that meant I had it for real. But Josh was piebald, parts of his skin black, parts white. That's real big power. Way more than mine."

Franco listened patiently.

"We was friends, you know? Other kids can smell power, like animals, they don't want to get too near it. Josh was worse off cause he looked funny, everybody always used to say his momma got him off a circus freak, or some show pony. It used to bother him, eat him up inside, I could feel it."

"Course, I didn't have many as would talk to me either, and the power didn't bother neither one of us, as we both had it. So we got to be real good friends."

Jeff smiled wistfully.

"He was real strong. He could make dead frogs come alive again. Make em croak and jump just like live ones. He could gentle wild beasts and untie knots with a thought, just like that," Jeff snapped his fingers.

"I remember one time Jimmy Deacon come running after us, we took off like a shot. But I looks over my shoulder and he's gainin' like the devil himself. Then suddenly he's tumbling like a dog in a barrel with his pants around his knees," Jeff laughed at the memory, "his belt come undone."

"He liked to call us 'Batman and Robin.' Me, I preferred to go by 'The Wizards of Huckleberry Finn.' We never told nobody, mind you, we was just together so it seemed good to have a together name."

"You were 'Robin'?" Franco asked.

Jeff did a mild 'aw shucks,' "The boy wonder, that was me."

"Why?"

Jeff frowned, "I guess on account of he thought of it, so he got to be 'Batman,' and his power was bigger."

Franco jotted some notes down. They didn't mean anything, they were just illegible doodles. The real notes he kept in his head.

"What about your power?"

"Weren't as strong," Jeff replied, "I could make a dead frog croak if I tried hard, and do knots with a bit of practice. I could do some things he couldn't, like get flashes of the future. I could read people real easy; he had to work at that. Course he was better at making them see or do things."

He laughed again.

"I remember one time he had Mary Ellen Stuart wallowing naked in a mud pit, just like a pig. There she was, the most stuck up girl in town; showing herself off like anything. I seen into her mind, and she didn't even know we were standing there watching. Far as she were concerned, she was having a fine bath behind locked doors in her daddy's big old tub."

He sobered.

"We didn't mean no harm with it though. Just fun was all."

Franco noted the mood shifts, he decided to probe.

"When did you start to mean harm?"

Jeff was startled.

"I never meant harm," he said.

The hell you didn't, thought Franco. Erma Louise Hampstead had been kidnapped and tortured for two and a half weeks in some bizarre satanic ritual; finally a heavy candle and brass holder, stolen from a church, had been rammed two and a half feet inside her with such force her heart had exploded. No harm, thought Franco.

"Really," said Jeff distantly, "we didn't mean no harm. Cept Joshua had a hard time of it, people had been down on him all his life and he was itching to give it back. But he wasn't bad, really."

Jeff paused, sober, remembering.

"Not till the sex thing anyway," he looked up at Franco. "We were getting older, you see. Getting these feelings. His were all twisted up. It was starting to twist up the rest of him too."

Abruptly, with a shake of his head, he seemed to change direction.

"Around that time we got us another friend. Sorel Hoke. She didn't have the power or anything. But nobody talked to her either, on account of her mother, May Hoke. Her mother was the local two-bit whore. Drunk all the time, did black folk and white trash, and anyone else with whiskey or money who weren't too particular about what they caught. Decent folk wouldn't associate with her or her daughter."

"Nobody wanted anything to do with Sorel, except the older boys who were turning her out just like her mother," He looked up, "imagine being so shit-out lonely and desperate that you'd let people do that to you."

"We talked to her. Sure, she smelled the power on us. But so what? She was so eaten out with needing that she was willing to be a hole just so they'd look at her and maybe say something while they was puttin' it in. Then there was us, who really talked to her, who treated her like a human being for maybe the first time in her life."

"We could have been Satan and his snake for all it mattered. She didn't care."

"For a while it got better. You know. The three of us were together all the time, except for when the two of them went off. She put up with what he did. Like I said, she was desperate, and I could just forget about it."

"So what happened?" Franco asked. But really, he already knew.

"She got pregnant," Jeff collected himself and then went on.

"At first Josh was real upset. But then he got to liking the idea. Said he'd make a real freak, to show people what one was. He said he was going to pack all kinds of power in it so it could take care of itself."

"I still liked him," Jeff asserted defensively, "but his sex thing was real twisted now, and it twisted up the rest of him. I didn't like to hang around him anymore."

"That was all right with him. He was going at Sorel every chance he got. You should have seen it, it weren't right, there she is, big as a cow, and he goin' right at her."

"It was like there was less and less of Sorel too. Used to be with us she talked like there was no tomorrow. Like she'd been saving up for years for someone to talk to," Jeff laughed, but it was a sour sound. "The bigger she got, the less she had to say. It was like she was being hollowed out from the inside."

"I didn't really understand. Probably cause I didn't want to," he said quietly, staring into space. "That's what it was."

"So what happened?" Franco asked. But it was just a formality, they both knew what happened.

"She died. The baby died," he said quietly. "Afterwards I came up on Josh at the river. I got him with a rock, he never saw it coming. Then I just held him under until he took a breath. It was simple as that."

Franco found it hard to breath. The session was over.

* * *

Franco was so edgy he put in too much money at the cigarette machine. It wouldn't give him change, so he put in more coins and got another pack.

"You all right?" Lieutenant Martins asked, coming up on him.

"Yeah," he said, he shoved both packs into his pockets.

"He's a sick one, isn't he."

"He killed Joshua LeBard."

"I'm not surprised; I've been going over the file that my agent sent up on it. Accidental death? My ass. There's holes there you could drive a truck through."

"You think it was covered up for some reason?" Franco asked.

Martins laughed.

"It's just a regular small town screw up. Ninety-nine times out of a hundred you have to put it down to messing up, not messing around. Never underestimate the power of incompetence."

"They just weren't paying attention to that one," Martins explained, "there'd been a really messy mother and child fatality that really smelled like a cover up, a couple of days before."

"Sorel Hoke," Franco said.

The lieutenant looked startled.

"If your man is still there; tell him to take a long hard look at that one."

"He already is. We are looking at every fatality and accident anywhere this bastard's ever been."

The detective leaned back against the wall.

"He has got to be the strangest serial killer anyone has ever seen," Martins said.

It seemed to Franco that Martins didn't really need a reply, he just wanted to talk.

"No patterns anywhere. Victims are male or female, white, black, whatever. As young as fourteen with the Mobley girl, or as old as seventy-nine like that guy Killian."

"The only thing that ties the homicides together is that he did them. Tyler Ridgefield was just a bar room brawl that got out of hand. But then you get Hampstead who's some weird satanic sacrifice. And what he did to the Mobley girl?"

They both shuddered.

"There is a pattern," Franco ventured.

"Yeah?"

"He got sicker each time."

"You know the one that gets me," Martins pulled a cigarette and lit it, puffing strongly, "it's the Jerry Killian thing that gets me."

Smoke got in Franco's face, he coughed.

Martins dropped the cigarette and ground it out under his foot.

"Sorry Doc."

Franco waved, "It's okay, I smoke them, I just don't breath them."

"Live longer that way," Martins laughed, then abruptly sobered. It disturbed Franco, the shift in mood reminded him of Jeffry. "The Killian thing. The one thing we know is that he stalks his victims, or enters into a relationship or something with them. Nobody ever sees them together, but everyone reports the victim's personality changes."

"So he stalks Killian. Right: There's these night attacks on a seventy-nine year old man. Breaks an arm. Couple of nights later breaks a leg. Just a classic sadistic maniac."

"A few weeks later he goes for the big one, breaks the spine. So then what happens?"

Martins began to pace. Franco had read the same reports, he knew, but Martins seemed to need to get it off his chest.

"I'll tell you what happens. The sick bastard drags Killian back to his own home and shacks up with him. He cooks for him, he cleans for him, he changes the frigging bedpans. He even does the frigging laundry."

"Killian lives two months before dying of accumulated effects of the injuries, and lack of treatment. Two weeks later the smell of rotting flesh overpowers the air fresheners, and the Super finds the body."

The lieutenant stopped in front of him to stab the air with his finger.

"The apartment was immaculate."

"I keep thinking about what it must have been like for Killian with this guy. One minute he is chopping him up by inches, the next minute, he's his goddamned mother."

"Twisted sex," Franco said. A moment of insight had dawned on him.

"What?"

"Most serial killers are twisted sex," Franco explained, "this one operates on twisted love."

The detective was silent for a few minutes, regarding him.

"And you have to talk to him," he said finally.

"Yes," Franco said, and shook his head.

"Jesus, Man," Martins said, "I'm sorry. I forgot."

Franco shrugged.

"Are you going to be all right?"

"Sure, I just need to unwind."

* * *

He went driving again. He didn't especially want to go home. He thought about writing a letter to his wife, but didn't feel up to it. He just cruised.

Once again, he found himself driving through the red light district, with all its garish come-ons. This time he drove slowly.

He stopped in front of a tall black hooker with braided dreadlocks. He wasn't sure what either of them were doing as she stepped up and he rolled down the window.

"You a cop?" she asked.

"No," he laughed involuntarily.

"Uh-huh," she surveyed him doubtfully. Abruptly she straightened and leaned forward resting her forearms against the top of his door.

She looked down at him.

"I bet if you weren't a cop, you'd like to touch me..." she looked nonchalantly up, "...somewhere."

This was a test, he realized. Her cleavage was hanging inches from his face. He reached out to touch the bare flesh, then emboldened by a moments whim, his hand slipped into the cup of her bra, grasped a nipple between thumb and forefinger.

Casually she stepped away from the car and walked around to the passenger's side. He barely got the door unlocked before she slid in next to him.

"Only two questions: What ya got and what ya want?"

Franco grinned suddenly, amused by her street accent. On the spur of the moment he decided to do his own black accent.

"I got what it takes," perhaps a rural accent, deep south rustic, he decided, "and ah got what yo needs."

She laughed.

The sex was simple animal. He did not care that she was completely uninvolved. All he wanted was her body, he'd had too much of other people's minds. He wanted to avoid that. He found he liked it that way.

Afterwards he went to use the can. When he came out, she was going through his wallet. She went for her purse. He got there first. He hit her in the face, her head snapped back thumping loudly against the wall.

I didn't hit her that hard, he thought wildly.

He picked up the purse. She sat there against the wall, watching him as he took the switchblade out. He popped the blade and then folded it. She gave nothing away.

Her nose was starting to bleed.

"Girl's got to make a living," she said nasally.

Still holding the purse and the blade, he got her a facecloth from the bathroom.

In front of her, he took fifty dollars in rumpled bills out and slipped them into his wallet.

"I screwed you, that cost me a hundred. You tried to screw me, that costs you fifty," he paused to see if she got it. "Fair?"

It amused him that he was still using his fake rural southern black accent. It made him feel tough.

"You got to learn to tell the players from the marks in this business, honey, or you just ain't going to last. Now: Fair?"

She seemed to consider it.

"Fair," she said.

* * *

The vague elation of the encounter was still with him when he returned to the station the next day. Martins was there to greet him.

"Hey bro," he said, using the accent. He felt like a kid with a shiny new toy.

Martins looked at him strangely for a moment, then shook it off.

"Before you go talk to our little psycho, are you ready for some twilight zone material?"

"Sure," He pronounced it as 'sho'.

There Are No Doors in Dark Places – Page 155

"Our man up that way is Dietrich. I sent him myself. Very thorough, very methodical, he misses nothing, but he has this habit of only passing on what you want. Sometimes, you have to ask twice."

"Go on," Franco encouraged.

"Well anyway, I told you we'd been looking at all the fatalities, and this one was no exception. Dietrich gets interested, but it doesn't seem to hook into our case, so he just sits on the stuff. Alright?"

"Uh huh."

"So last night I called up and asked for all of it: Get this: Definitely a cover up. The daughter of the town tramp gets knocked up, either tries to induce an abortion in the seventh month, or goes into premature labor. Doctor rushes over. Loses them both. Coroner exonerates everyone."

"It happens," Franco commented.

"The Doctor becomes a chronic alcoholic, or maybe after that he just isn't hiding it so well. Career lasts another two years then he's in a sanitarium until he dies."

"So you think the Doctor had a problem before this happened, on that night his luck ran out, and the loyal townsfolk covered for him?" Franco asked.

"Could be, but it gets better. There was an attending police officer. That night, he discharged his service revolver. Six shots. Inside that house, apparently."

"You're kidding."

"His report says he attended at a medical emergency and wound up emptying his pistol at a rabid raccoon in the back yard. Good story, but he can't seem to explain how he saw the raccoon in the back yard when there were no lights. Or why he seemed to be shooting from inside the house. Or even whether he fired before, after, or during the medical emergency."

"Now, listen to this. All rabid animal sightings, and all suspect carcasses, go to the state veterinary examiner. The only rabies report they've ever received out of that county is thirty years old."

"So go ask the officer?"

"Can't. Six years ago he's sitting at a speed trap, he puts the gun in his mouth and blows the top of his head off. A couple of kids on picnic see it all. No question, suicide."

"So what do you make of it?"

"The rabies story is crap. He emptied his gun into something, I have no idea what, but it wasn't a raccoon."

Martins paused and took a deep breath.

"Dietrich felt to me like he was holding out. So I told him to give it all to me. Here's where it gets weird: The listed weight of the newborns death certificate was forty-two pounds."

"Get out of here," Franco scoffed, "physically impossible. Off by a factor of ten."

"True," Martins admitted, "someone scratched out forty-two and wrote in four and a half. But the original number was forty-two."

"Dietrich kept on," the Detective told him, "The mother, Sorel Hoke's weight on the death certificate was less than half what she'd weighed at the six month stage at her last check up."

"The grandmother, May Hoke, has been institutionalized ever since that night. Catatonic."

"You couldn't have gotten this last night, you're pulling my leg," Franco scoffed.

"This is straight up, like I said: Dietrich's been digging on his own. Want to visit the grave? You can't, none of the churches in town would allow either the mother or the baby into their cemeteries. Instead, they were buried in unconsecrated ground. Get this: In separate locations."

"Everyone seems to have forgotten where they were buried. Neither of the two mortuaries has any record or recollection of doing the embalming, but one of them must have. There aren't even records for the pallbearers or the gravedigger."

"Rural legends," Franco scoffed, "every small town has a skeleton in its closet and a monster in its grave."

"Sure they do," Martins admitted, "most of them evaporate when you start to dig. But not this one. This just gets more solid the harder you go at it."

"So, what are you saying?" Franco laughed. "Sorel Hoke gave birth to a monster baby? The Officer fired six shots to stop it? Everyone involved is dead or out of it, and everyone else just swept it under a carpet?"

"I'm not saying anything," Martins answered, "I don't know enough. All I know is something weird happened, and it seems to tie into your boy somehow. It's like there is something dangerous and messed up and mindless floating around, maybe it started there and our boy has been carrying it around ever since."

"Thanks for the insight," Franco told him.

The Detective paled momentarily. He put his hand out and grasped Franco's arm.

"I'm sorry Doc. I apologize. I keep forgetting that you have to deal with him. This stuff screws up the rest of us as it is."

"It's okay."

"You take care of yourself in there, alright."

* * *

Lose the accent, Franco told himself. It's time to put away the toys. Jeff looked up.

"So why did you kill Joshua that first time?" he asked abruptly.

"I had to. I could see the future," he responded.

I bet you did, you sick little faggot. Franco thought.

Jeff abruptly blushed and looked down.

"I mean, it was like I told you. I'd get these flashes of the future. Of things that could be. This was just the start. Josh was going to do a lot of stuff. Horrible stuff. I had to stop him."

Franco felt abruptly tired.

"No more of these cheap dime novel fantasies, Jeff. Neither one of us needs them. You had a thing for Josh. He got a thing for Sorel. End of Batman and Robin. You didn't like that. So you messed up the pregnancy somehow. Maybe it was as easy as getting the doctor drunk enough to screw it up. But then Josh still doesn't come back, so you kill him."

He paused.

"Maybe Josh figured it out, or was going to. Maybe all that bad stuff you could 'see' Josh doing in the future: Maybe all that boiled down to Josh putting it all together and coming looking for you. How am I doing so far?"

Jeff was silent, looking at him.

Franco went on.

"So you go away, but you can't make it work. You keep trying to hook up with different people, as different as you can find. Maybe it works for a while, but then it starts to go wrong. You start losing it. They remind you of Josh. You kill them."

"Tell me Jeff," Franco asked, "does this sound like real life? Does it sound like your life?"

Franco was conscious of having said it as much for his own benefit as for Jeff. He felt a need to drag Jeff into the real world before his fantasy world dragged Franco down.

Jeff said nothing. He just looked at Franco. The seconds yawned into minutes, the minutes grew into a bridge of silence.

Finally, Franco gave in.

There Are No Doors in Dark Places – Page 159

"All right then, let's do 'Return of the Jedi.' You killed Joshua. How come you have to keep on killing him? And why do you keep...changing the way you kill them?"

Jeff said nothing.

"Tell me about Tyler?" Franco prompted gently.

Jeff licked his lips, almost biting them.

"Josh was real powerful, like I said. Power like that just don't die. Josh became a ha'nt," Jeff said.

For a delirious moment Franco thought that he'd said Josh had turned into an ant. The image was so ludicrous. Then he translated it again: Ha'nt, Haunt.

"Haunt. You mean a ghost?" Franco asked.

Jeff seemed to consider the notion.

"Sort of like that, yeah. I didn't know for two years. I'd feel sumthin from time to time. But with the power, you feel lots of things."

"I only knew when Tyler came at me when I was shooting pool. I took a real close look at him. Like this:" Jeff gave Franco a brief stare that went right through him, it left him shivering, feeling alone and naked, "Tyler was gone. Josh was inside. He tried to do me, but I done him again instead. Then I ran."

"Why did you run?" Franco asked softly.

"Ha'nts don't move about so well in the material world. They can't find their way easy, especially if you go a ways. I figured I'd leave Josh way behind, he'd settle down without me to stir him up."

"What about the police?" Franco asked.

Jeff looked at him with wide uncomprehending eyes and shook his head. He had never run from the police. Of course. In spite of himself, Franco was impressed by the strength of the delusional structure.

"I settled down someplace new and started seeing this girl called Elly Soames. She started seeing me actually, but I didn't

figure out what that might mean, until she took me down to
the river. She said we'd get it on there. Then she pulled the
knife as we were doing it."

"Joshua again?" Franco asked.

Elly Soames, raped, drowned, stabbed twenty five times,
head and parts of her body crushed under thirty pound rocks.

"It was like them frogs I told you about. They'd be dead,
but he'd make em get up and sing. I had a real hard time with
her. After that, I learned to watch out for him."

"Tell me, what happened to Tyler? Where was he when
Josh was inside him?" Franco inquired.

"Gone," Jeff said "I wasn't sure before. But now I think
he replaces them bit by bit. Like in a petrified tree, little bits
of rock start replacing the wood, until you turn around and
look at your forest and it's all stone. I think now, they just
stop existing."

"You think that now?"

"Yeah."

"Not before?"

"No." He looked vaguely haunted; Franco noted with
satisfaction, some human guilt was finally starting to show
through.

"I thought maybe," Jeff said softly, "I could drive him out.
Let the original persons come back."

"Erma Louise Hampstead," Franco whispered. A forty
four year old mother of three children who lived in a suburb
with her engineer husband and two Irish setters. Erma, who
had never so much as had a parking ticket. Erma whose heart
had exploded when a holy object had been forced so far into
her body that her diaphragm had ruptured.

"I tried to exorcise them. I figured I had the power. Maybe
I could do it. But it didn't work."

Franco nodded. It was a sick joke. Not a satanic ritual. An exorcism. Not that it made much difference to Erma Louise Hampstead.

"So what happened after that?"

"I learned," Jeff said, "that he couldn't get out of bodies as easy as he could get into them. He'd have to wait until they died before the flesh would let go its hold on him."

"So you started crippling them?" Franco said.

"Seemed like the best thing," Jeff admitted. "Of course, dealing with ha'nts, it's hard to tell where to draw the line. The spirit can make flesh work, even if it's broken."

"And they tended to die anyway. It just took longer." Franco commiserated.

"Yeah, but while it was happening, I was safe. I didn't need to worry about him coming up behind me. I could talk to him. Try and reason him down." Jeff said.

"That was good of you," Franco said dryly, Jeff didn't notice the sarcasm.

"But it must have been hard to talk to Josh if you were piercing his eardrums?" Franco couldn't help thinking about what had been done to the Mobley girl.

"Had to," Jeff explained, "a ha'nt on its own don't cause too much trouble, no matter how much power it's got. It can't see the material world enough to focus properly. But a ha'nt with some flesh wrapped around it is different. If it can see the material world through flesh eyes, or hear through ears, even walk around with a busted body, there's no telling what it could get up to."

"So that's the Mobley girl. You were afraid she was going to get up and walk around after you broke her neck, so you decided to be safe and break her legs. Then you were still afraid, so you tied her up," Franco said.

Jeff nodded.

"I told you about them frogs."

"You did," Franco agreed.

"You don't believe me," Jeff said softly.

Franco thought it over before answering.

"I think we both know what really happened," he said softly. "But for what it's worth: I believe that you believe what you've told me. I believe you need to believe it. I believe it's how you live with it."

He stood up and walked to the door.

He turned back, to look at Jeff. The youth raised his face to look at him.

"May God have mercy on your soul," Franco said, almost compassionately.

* * *

"That sick pathological demented monster," Lieutenant Martin spoke slowly, without heat or emphasis.

"It's finished," Franco said. He felt immense relief.

"Now it's just tying up loose ends."

"Not my job," Franco said.

"You did more than I'd ask any man to do. Are you going to be all right?"

Franco shrugged.

"Sho nuff, need to unwind tha's all."

"Yeah, I noticed you quit smoking."

"Thousands of times," Franco laughed. He decided to buy a pack, just to demonstrate.

"Where'd you get the Louisiana accent?"

"TV ah guess. Mebbe da five an dime."

"Helps with the tension?"

"Yeah."

"I know," Martins sympathized, "back when I was in high school some kid started doing a British accent. Then someone else caught a Marx Brothers movie and started doing Chico's Italian accent. Before you knew it, it was all over the place. It would die down, then someone would

There Are No Doors in Dark Places – Page 163

figure out how to do a new accent, and it would start up again."

Martins shook his head, "I'll tell you, just before a dance or an exam, we sounded like the United Nations."

They both laughed.

"By the way, I think you're right about the Hoke thing," the Detective told him, "Our psycho's dad was the town bootlegger. I figure the kid did runs for the old man."

"We have an alcoholic doctor who needs to be fairly liquored to work. He gets called to an emergency, he needs booze to cope. The kid delivers. Maybe he just ups the proof a bit, the Doc takes way too much, or maybe he spikes it with acid, who knows?"

"Things start going wrong: The Doctor is freaking out, the grandma is freaking out, the mom is screaming her lungs out, the patrolman panics and shoots up the house. Who knows, maybe he plugged the mom or kid? Maybe it didn't make a difference by that time?"

"End of the night, you got two dead bodies and some solid reputations about to go down the toilet. Town fathers think to themselves: 'Hey, it's only the slut and the slut in training.' End of story."

"That's plausible." Franco agreed.

"Yeah, it's only closer to home that gets hard. Did you hear: Charles Mobley committed suicide the other day?"

"The last victim's father. That's terrible." Franco said.

"Yeah, tell me about it. Seems the little girl was turning into a shit before the psycho even hit town. Drugs, promiscuity, violence."

"Violence?" Franco asked.

"Seems she rat-tailed one of her little friends. We're only just putting it together."

"Rat-Tailed," Franco repeated quizzically.

"Sure, you know those cheap plastic combs, the ones with the long narrow handle that comes to a point?"

"Sure. Everyone has one of those."

"Hold it by the comb part, your handle becomes a stiletto, strike hard enough it'll go right into a person, there's your rat-tail."

"Christ. The things people will do," Franco murmured in disgust.

"You said it," Martins affirmed. "the Mobley girl, she comes right up beside this kid in the school washroom. Spears her through the kidney just like that. Walks away."

"That's sick."

"This was a sick girl. Autopsy confirmed all kinds of drugs, crack, coke, heroin, speed, acid, in trace amounts. Apparently she'd been doing real heavy before her encounter. She also had some healthy cases of syphilis and gonorrhea."

"Lovely," Franco said, he really didn't want to hear it. Dealing with Jeff had been enough.

"Want to know the sickest part: It seems her dad had identical strains of syphilis and gonorrhea."

"Makes sense," Franco said, "parental sexual abuse is often associated with children acting out like that."

"Here's the kicker. They typed the case developments. Turns out that he didn't give it to her, she gave it to him."

Franco felt an almost physical nausea. Abruptly he stood and started walking away.

"Sick justice that she ran into the psycho," Martins finished, "but I wouldn't wish what he did to her on my worst enemy."

* * *

In the car, a migraine began to cascade. He rubbed his temples.

"Oh lordy. Oh lordy," he murmured. He smiled vaguely; amused that he was still doing the accent.

There Are No Doors in Dark Places – Page 165

Beer. He needed a beer.

He stopped at three liquor stores before he found one that sold a decent brand of beer. A half decent beer, he thought, was that too much to ask? While there, as an afterthought he remembered his silent promise and bought another pack of cigarettes.

He got home, slouching into the living room. He threw the pack on the coffee table with the others, popped a beer and flopped onto the couch.

He half sat, half lay there, sipping the beer. Staring at the coffee table.

What's wrong with this picture? He thought.

Gradually, it came to him.

There are three unopened packs of cigarettes sitting on the coffee table.

I smoke two packs a day, for the last fifteen years.

There are three unopened packs of cigarettes sitting on the coffee table.

When was the last time I had a cigarette?

He felt cold suddenly. Jeff's words ran through his mind.

"Josh takes over people."

A rational part of him asserted itself.

"Occupational hazard," he said out loud, to comfort himself, "Put a psychiatrist in a room with a man who thinks he's Napoleon for a year. Open the door. Maybe you've got two sane rational well-adjusted men. Maybe you have two guys with their hands in their shirts."

"Ah don need to accept dis dilusion," he said.

Stopping smoking wasn't proof of anything. He'd probably had lots of other periods where he'd simply not bothered to smoke and hadn't noticed because he was busy or distracted. Smoking didn't mean anything.

Why do I keep talking like a Louisiana Negro?

I'm faithful to my wife.

I just slept with a prostitute.

I beat a woman.

I never did anything like that in my life.

He paused, letting the thought slide into his mind.

So why did it feel like I'd been doing it for years?

I don't even drink beer.

He held the can up to inspect it carefully for the first time. An Alabama brand. He threw it across the room; spilling beer arced from the can, soaking into the carpet. He hurled the rest of them at the wall.

This is nuts. He thought. Don't give in to the delusion. If you were being possessed you'd feel it.

Wouldn't you?

"It happens a piece at a time," Jeff had said. "Like fossilization, one substance being imperceptibly transformed into another, replaced by another."

Call my wife. He thought. He was starting to sweat. He could feel panic running under his skin.

He couldn't remember her phone number.

Don't panic. Happens to people all the time. Too many digits. Everyone forgets phone numbers. Even if you can't remember them, they are easy enough to find.

So: What's her name?

He couldn't remember.

He stood there, suddenly drenched in his own sweat. What the hell is her name?

He bolted for the mantlepiece. There was the wedding picture. There she is. There's no names on it. What sort of moron takes wedding pictures and doesn't put their names on it, he wanted to scream. He hurled the picture away. He tore at the mantelpiece, looking for clues.

The photo albums. At least he remembered where they were. He tore across the room, ripping open the cabinet. There they were. Flip. Flip. Flip. Pictures. Pictures. Didn't anyone ever bother to sign the damned things? What about future generations, he thought irritably, how were they to know who these people were? How am I supposed to know?

There! The wedding invitation! His hands were shaking so badly he tore the cardboard. It said: Marilyn.

He fell back, leaning against the wall. Marilyn, he thought. Marilyn. Marilyn. He crumpled the invitation, holding it against his sweating chest, feeling his heart pound.

It's going to be all right, he thought. Marilyn.

It's just a delusional attack. Occupational hazard.

Marilyn. It was like a holy word. Marilyn. It would keep him safe. Marilyn.

Eats away. Jeff had said. Insidiously. Replacing.

No. Marilyn.

He got to his feet and walked to the bedroom. That's it. Get closer to her. Marilyn.

He looked into the dresser mirror.

He felt a profound shock. It wasn't a familiar face. It was the face that looked back at him all his life.

It wasn't familiar any more.

He clutched the wedding invitation to himself and approached the mirror. Marilyn, he thought, it was a plea.

No.

It was all right. Stubble. He rubbed his chin. Taking comfort in the thick black hairs. Stubble. I haven't been shaving lately. He watched himself rubbing his chin. I'm not used to looking like this.

This should be white. He thought, while rubbing his chin. The lower jaw should be white, not black and stubble. That's a white part.

The rest of my face is black, he thought, except for one patch around the right eye, and another high up by the hairline.

He smashed the mirror with his fist.

He backed away slowly. His hand was bleeding.

That was good. The pain helped clear his mind.

"Get out," he said the words out loud. He was pleased at how articulate and reasonable they sounded.

"GET OUT!" he screamed aloud.

"GET OUT OF ME NOW!" he roared in his mind.

He raced for the bathroom. There was a mirror there. He smashed it. Good.

Shower. Good. Hot water. To the max. All the way. Burn the ghost out.

He waited as long as he dared for the water to get hot. Almost four minutes. He stripped off his clothes and stepped into it.

The agony took his breath away.

"Get out," he gasped. It became a mantra, he said it over and over again as he moved himself under the shower.

His skin turned red. It scalded. It blistered.

Not enough. He leaped from the shower, staggering blindly, walking across shards of broken mirror. He fell a couple of times. He didn't care.

What was his name?

Marilyn.

He held that to him.

"Get out," he whispered over and over.

He found the kitchen. Yes. He turned the stove on. All the elements. Yes. That would do it.

All he had to do was wait. He couldn't wait. He ransacked the cutlery drawer. Knives. Yes. To pass the time. To make it get out.

The floor was getting slippery. The stove was finally ready. The elements were a cheerful friendly red.

"Get out," he told it aloud. A last warning. No answer.

Fine then. He'd show it that he meant business.

He placed both hands on the two elements. He heard blood sizzling, smelled his own flesh cooking. The pain was unendurable. He bit his lip to keep from screaming. He danced naked in front of the stove as if it was a pagan god, and he writhing in religious ecstasy before it.

It wasn't enough, he thought, through the thickening smoke.

All right then, he thought, no more Mister Nice Guy.

He began to bend forward, lowering himself towards another element. He could feel it resisting. He would not yield. Inches away from the glowing red element, a tear drop fell and sizzled instantly to oblivion.

This time he really did scream.

* * *

When it was all over, really over, he called Lieutenant Martins.

* * *

Jeff looked up from his cell. He was startled to see Doctor Franco staring down at him, a guard by his side.

Half the Doctors face was swathed in bandages. His hands were similarly wrapped. He moved stiffly.

"You're being transferred to Fillmore Psychiatric. They have facilities for you there," Franco gritted.

Jeff didn't say anything.

"The papers are all in order. Let's get moving." He turned and stalked off. Jeff and the guard had to scramble to keep up. Franco stalked through the institution like an angry ghost.

The guard left them at the gate that lead to the parkade. Franco continued to stride forward. Jeff hopped along to keep pace.

"I despise you. You little shit," Franco snarled.

"You wrecked my life," he said, he savored the words for a second, and said it again. "You wrecked my life."

"But I believe now. Do you know that?"

"Yes," Jeff answered.

"I believe now. In 'ha'nts', stinking ghosts that follow you around and possess people," he gritted.

"It almost took me. Did you know that?" Franco spat.

"No," Jeff said, hopping desperately to keep up as Franco sped along.

"But I fought it off."

Franco stopped abruptly. Jeff almost ran into him. He loomed over Jeff.

"I never want to see or hear of you again for as long as I live. Do you understand, you verminous faggot cretin?"

"Yes," Jeff replied.

Franco turned and was striding again, he seemed to barely contain himself.

"There is no Fillmore Psychiatric," Franco spat, "you are going to disappear, and you are going to take your 'ha'nt' with you. Understand?"

Franco didn't wait for the reply; they had come to the end of the parkade. There was a car waiting.

"My life will be over. But I will never have to deal with you or your stinking ghost again. Do we understand each other?" he gritted.

"Yes," Jeff said.

Franco walked him to the car. He opened the back passenger door. Jeff slid in. The driver turned to regard him.

"This is Lieutenant Martins. You've wrecked his life too. He'll take you somewhere, and then you are on your own. Understand."

"Yes," Jeff answered, and then ventured, "thank you."

"Go to hell," Franco snarled.

He stalked away.

They watched him vanish into the distance of the grey parkade.

Finally Lieutenant Martins turned to regard Jeff for the first time.

"It takes me a while, but I learn from you, Jeff. You don't need to go straight at things. A push here, a push there, it gets the job done."

Jeff was startled for a moment, then he looked real hard.

His face broke into a huge sunny grin.

"Joshua!"

The End

Voices

The nurse bustled in on her morning rounds.

Good morning Mister Hersh," she said with measured cheer. "How are we feeling today?"

"Morning nurse," Hersh replied softly.

"Good morning, I'm fine," Hersh's cancer said brightly. The nurse couldn't hear it speak, of course.

When the cancer had started to speak, Hersh had often replied out loud. He soon discovered that no one else heard the voice. Now, he just spoke to it with his mind.

The cancer hadn't quite caught on though, it still responded to voices that never answered back to it.

"Did you sleep well?" the Nurse asked.

Hersh shrugged.

She measured out Hersh's drugs in a little paper cup.

"These will make you feel better," she told him.

They didn't. They didn't actually dull the pain. What they seemed to do was to fuzz his mind. Make him a little less cognizant, a little less lucid. Less able to appreciate pain and nausea.

Hersh swallowed the pills, intimately conscious of his tongue moving in his mouth, of his throat gulping.

He wallowed from the glass of water that the nurse handed him.

The cancer watched these procedures with rapt interest.

After the nurse left, he laid back in the hospital bed.

"So," asked the cancer, "what are we going to be doing today?"

"I haven't decided," Hersh replied. "Maybe we'll go horseback riding, or fly a plane."

"Cool," the cancer replied enthusiastically.

Hersh suspected that the cancer had no idea what he was talking about. Sometimes, it seemed to have little grasp of the external world. But that was all right, it was always enthusiastic.

Sometimes Hersh thought his cancer had more life than he did.

It had little grasp of irony, and except when he felt it rummaging in his memories, it only heard what he spoke to it, or spoke aloud. He could tell it anything.

It couldn't, or perhaps wouldn't, read his mind.

"Or we could watch television?"

"Sesame Street!" squeaked his cancer.

But it was too late for that, so they watched game shows.

Hersh lay in the hospital bed, with his cancer, watching the Wheel of Fortune.

Every now and then it would ask a question. It seemed to have trouble understanding Vanna White's role. Hersh explained things as best he could.

His cancer seemed to prefer Jeopardy, but that wouldn't be on for another hour.

* * *

Perhaps it was the drugs that constantly fogged his mind, but he couldn't quite remember when his cancer had started talking to him.

He had, until his illness, lived a solitary and unexceptional life of quiet reserve. It had never really bothered him. He'd grown older as his friends settled down and married and drifted away. He would receive cards denoting the birth of children, and would methodically put them in the same box he kept the condolences cards from his parents' funerals.

It was not an exciting existence, but it hadn't been unpleasant.

Until one morning when he found himself helplessly, spastically coughing blood into the toilet.

Then his spare and Spartan existence had become intolerable. He'd faced his illness alone for a while, discovering his life was a void. Finally he'd checked into the hospital.

A few people sent cards. His office sent flowers.

Nobody visited.

Hersh sat in the hospital bed and watched television. He did crossword puzzles and read magazines and played solitaire. The nurses bustled around him with distracted impersonal efficiency.

His life boiled down to time killing exercises sitting alone in a room in a fog of drugs and pain as the cancer took over his life.

He didn't remember when he'd started talking to it.

Why shouldn't he talk to it?

People talked to their cats, their plants, to the people and things in their lives. He'd never had cats or plants, never really had anything to talk to. Why shouldn't he talk to it?

What else was there left for him to talk to?

It had slipped unbidden into his life, like an unwanted guest, slowly wrecking the home it visited.

All he knew, really, was that he had been talking to it for such a long time that he hadn't been at all surprised when it started talking to him.

* * *

They were sitting out in the Hospital gardens, Hersh and his Doctor. The staff thought it was good for the patients to get some fresh air once in a while.

There Are No Doors in Dark Places – Page 175

Hersh sat in the Gomers area, old men and terminal patients who sat quietly where they had been placed. Over on the other side of the gardens, he could hear children playing.

The cancer, fascinated, wanted him to go over there.

Hersh sat where he was.

"I hear voices," Hersh told the Doctor.

"Whose?" the cancer asked, fascinated.

"My cancer," Hersh told the Doctor, "I think it's talking to me."

"I am talking to you," the cancer said, mildly offended.

The Doctor stared at Hersh with mild surprise. He was a short young man with a head of curly hair. He was much younger than Hersh, which made it difficult for him to be authoritative. He compensated with a restrained playfulness.

"What does it say?"

"I dunno," Hersh gestured vaguely. "We talk about television and stuff."

"Uh huh," said the Doctor, "so it's not telling you that you're the messiah or anything like that?"

Hersh shook his head.

"It isn't suggesting that you kill your Doctor?" There was a trace of a smile in the Doctor's eyes.

"I wouldn't," the cancer said, indignant.

"No," Hersh admitted, smiling a little.

"Well, that's something anyway," the Doctor said cheerily. He examined his chart. "Have you ever had auditory hallucinations before?"

"What's that?" the cancer piped. Hersh ignored it. Sometimes, if he left it alone, it seemed able to figure things out for itself, as if it was rummaging in the back of his brain for information.

"No."

"Anyone in your family ever been diagnosed with schizophrenia or psychosis of any sort?"

"No."

"You ever experimented with drugs when you were young? Strong ones like LSD, Peyote, mushrooms?"

"Some grass."

"Grass?" the cancer asked confused. An image of golf course greens drifted through his mind.

"I'll explain later," Hersh told it.

"Grass wouldn't do it." The Doctor shook his head. "Any childhood traumas?"

"No."

"Have you ever had any other strange experiences? Reincarnation flashbacks? Religious experiences? Alien abductions? Ever seen a ghost?"

"No. None of that."

"So," said the Doctor, "what you're saying is that you're perfectly normal, except that you have cancer and it's talking to you."

"Is that possible?"

The Doctor shrugged.

"Lots of people wind up hearing voices, for one reason or another. It's just one part of the brain talking to the other, and because of injury or illness it sounds like someone else.

"More likely it's a side effect of the medication, or something else entirely."

The Doctor gave the ghost of an impish smile.

"But you never know. They've found tumors that had developed hair and teeth."

"Really?" the cancer asked, fascinated.

"I didn't know that," Hersh said, "I thought it was just... a growth, like a boil or something."

"Basically, cancers are just cells gone wild. But they're still cells that contain all your DNA, your biological map for everything. So, sometimes you get cancers that seem to form complicated structures, like hair or teeth."

"Neat," said the cancer. Hersh could tell that it was impressed.

"But it's almost always malformed and unusable. It's rogue cells multiplying and dying, throwing out random bits of DNA instruction."

"It could develop a brain then?" Hersh asked.

"The idea of cancer cells assembling into something as complex as a thinking organ is so improbable it's ludicrous. It's like a handful of metal shavings assembling themselves into a Rolex.

"I mean, it's just barely remotely possible, but I doubt it." The Doctor smiled again. "Remember: When in doubt, go with the simpler explanation."

"So what do I do?" Hersh asked.

"About the voices?" the Doctor replied. "Well, as long as they aren't telling you that you can fly, or that you should shoot the hospital staff, I wouldn't worry about it.

"We can deal with it later. Right now, we should be concerned with saving your life."

"Okay," Hersh said.

He watched the Doctor walk off.

"He's nice," said the cancer, "I like him."

Hersh nodded.

* * *

Later on, they were doing a crossword together.

The cancer wasn't very good at it. It had a tendency to invent words, as if its experience encompassed foreign dimensions. But once in a while, he could feel it shuffle through his memories and dredge up a correct answer that had eluded Hersh. So, he let it play.

The cancer asked a question.

"Hey Dad," it said.

"Hmmm," Hersh mumbled out loud.

"What did the Doctor mean when he talked about saving your life?"

Odd question, Hersh thought to himself.

"It means I'm dying," he told the cancer.

SHOCK!

The cancer was silenced for an instance. Its palpable surprise and horror radiated through him.

"Oh Dad," it whispered in his mind. "What's happening to you?"

"You are," he told it.

"What?"

Confusion.

"You're killing me."

There was a sudden violence inside him, as if his memories were thrown open, desperately leaved through for terrible corroboration.

It screamed.

Inside, he felt it rushing away, withdrawing in on itself.

Silence.

Hersh waited a moment. It's now familiar presence was absent from his mind.

"You there?" he asked experimentally.

No answer.

After a while, Hersh went back to his crossword puzzle, though he didn't do nearly as well.

After that, he went to sleep.

* * *

Hersh had a dream. In it, the cancer came to him, all red and bashful, and it spoke.

"Uh... Hello Dad," it said. "Listen, I've been doing some looking around, and you're right... about... it."

It seemed to wring its metaphorical hands in frustration.

"I'm sorry. I never meant to hurt you. I never meant for you to suffer. I just never realized...

"I mean, I was young and growing and growing and growing and I just figured that nothing bad would ever happen. You know how it is? You're young and growing and you assume that everything will last forever, that the world will be infinite? You don't realize that there are limits, or what happens when you press those limits.

"I feel terrible, I feel awful. I'm really sorry. I love you Dad. You know I'd never do anything to hurt you."

"Anyway, I want you to know I'm going to make things right. After all, I live here too. I've been looking around in here, and I think I can fix it.

"It's not hard, just retard a little growth here, spur some there, move some hormones, adjust a balance, tweak the immune system a bit. Pretty straightforward actually, I just assumed you handled these things yourself, but it looks like you've mostly got it all on automatic.

"I think I can make a few improvements actually. I'm thinking of doing something with all the cholesterol around your heart. Maybe it's supposed to be there, but I really think things would work better without it. You'll never be sick again, Dad, never in pain. I promise. And you'll live a long long time, maybe forever, and you won't ever get old.

"You handle the outside, I'll take care of the inside. We'll be a great team, Dad. I swear.

"I want to make things better for you, Dad. I want to show you that I appreciate what you've gone through for me. We'll be a family, Dad. We'll be terrific together."

Hersh could feel it go silent, waiting expectantly for his answer. He tried to smile at it, to say something. But instead, he just drifted off to sleep.

* * *

The next morning, Hersh woke feeling much better.

The pain was gone entirely. Hersh had a new sense of energy, of wellbeing.

There Are No Doors in Dark Places – Page 180

"Hi Dad," the cancer said brightly. "How do you feel?"

"Pretty good," Hersh said out loud.

"We're glad," the cancer replied.

"I think we'll go for a walk," Hersh said out loud.

"That sounds like fun," the cancer said.

* * *

"Why aren't we eating today?" the cancer asked curiously.

"Hush," Hersh told it.

The Doctor was in the room, talking to him.

"Still hearing voices?" the Doctor asked, noticing.

"Now and then," Hersh replied carefully.

The Doctor shrugged his shoulders. "We'll see about dealing with that afterwards."

"Surgery is scheduled for 3:00 pm. With any luck, it'll be a simple procedure," he continued. "Just remember the precautions."

"All right," Hersh answered.

"Any questions?"

Hersh shook his head.

"Fine," said the Doctor, "I'll see you tomorrow when you're post-op. I'm really pleased to see the improvements you've made recently."

After the Doctor left, the cancer spoke up again.

"What was that all about?" it asked.

"It's the operation."

"What operation?"

That stopped Hersh for a moment. Could it really not know? It occurred to him then, that it had never really thought of itself as a disease, but rather, some sort of progeny of his.

His child.

What a natural mistake, he thought. Picking and choosing concepts haphazardly from his mind. Grappling with language. Struggling with concepts of an outside world alien

There Are No Doors in Dark Places – Page 181

to it. Was it a surprise, as it forged a self-identity, that it would equate itself, not with disease and illness, but with people?

It was waiting politely for his reply.

Hersh felt embarrassed suddenly.

"My operation," he told it. "They're going to cut me open."

"Why?" the cancer asked.

"The cure for cancer," he said, "cut it out."

SHOCK! Again, like before, the vast ripple of surprise and trepidation. Then suddenly the familiar sensation of it desperately plunging through his memories. Sorting, selecting, collating.

An instant of heart pounding silence.

SCREAM ringing through him. A scream of shock and horror, or a world turned inside out.

And at the center of it all, a sensation of betrayal.

* * *

"You fucker," it screamed. "Fucker! Prick! Bastard!"

Hersh closed his eyes trying to blot it out, but that only made the screaming worse in his head. Giddy and exhausted from the drugs, he could only lay there and listen as it raged.

"I can't believe you'd do this to me, your own flesh and blood! I loved you, you bastard, and now you're going to open us up and cut me out. Oh Jesus, please don't do this to me. I'll do anything. You're killing the both of us. Oh please."

"It won't be long now, Mister Hersh," the intern whispered to him as they wheeled him into the operating room. Hersh blinked in acknowledgement.

"Oh God," the cancer said desperately. "Why doesn't somebody stop this?"

But nobody heard it.

"You bastard," the cancer screamed anew, "you total bastard. You never loved me, you probably never even liked me, and now you're going to do this thing to me. I'm going to get you. I could have done so much for you, we could have done so much together. But you have to be alone, you selfish pig.

"Don't you dare think you can just cut me out and walk away. I'm going to get you. I'm going to make you pay."

As the anesthesia mask closed over his face, the last thing he heard was his cancer, desperately howling revenge.

* * *

On the table, Hersh had a dream. He dreamed that his cancer spoke to him one last time, just before they cut it out.

It said: "Please Dad, I love you. Why didn't you love me?"

Hersh wanted to say that he did, to explain. But it was gone. He realized that he couldn't explain, anyway.

* * *

Hersh woke. The pain, his old friend, was back. But this was a different pain. A pain of sutures and incisions, of a body grossly violated rather than insidiously decaying.

He contemplated this pain for a few minutes and decided that it was a good thing. He felt the vague fuzz of drugs in his mind and this inspired a feeling of wrongness.

He tried to track it down. Ah yes, it was silent inside. No voices. Where was the voice? Then he remembered that the cancer had been cut out. Satisfied, he drifted back to sleep.

* * *

Time passed.

The Doctor came to visit, he sat beside the bed.

"How are you feeling?" the Doctor asked.

"Fine," replied Hersh. "Tired."

How should he feel? He'd been dying and they'd gutted him like a trout to save his life. How do you feel for something like that?

It was quiet in his head. He found himself asking questions or explaining things to the emptiness. He missed

There Are No Doors in Dark Places – Page 183

the curious childlike voice he'd ascribed to the cancer. His cancer.

"You're recovering nicely," the Doctor said genially. "We got most of it."

"Most," Hersh asked quietly.

There was a silence in his mind.

"Tell me about the tumor," he asked.

The Doctor looked surprised at the question.

"It was just a tumor. Gray pink. It looked kind of like a cauliflower, wrinkled up like a brain."

"Like a brain," Hersh repeated.

The Doctor frowned.

"It wasn't a brain, it was just a tumor. Just cells growing wild and uncontrolled."

"I've heard," Hersh whispered, "that they've found tumors that had hair and teeth."

"It was just a tumor," the Doctor said emphatically. "The biopsy will show it. It was just a mass or renegade cells."

That called me 'Dad,' Hersh thought bitterly.

Biopsy? An undefinable unease swept through him.

"Just make sure no one touches it," Hersh said. "Okay?"

He wanted to tell the Doctor to give it a decent burial, but he knew how that would sound.

"We need to talk about something else," the Doctor said.

"No," Hersh said quickly.

"The tumor had metastasized. There was a secondary tumor."

"You didn't get that one too?"

"Not from where we opened you up. It's not like lifting the hood of a car; we try and minimize the degree of intervention. From the surgery, we could see evidence of it; we just weren't in a position to remove it."

"Oh," said Hersh.

Back to the battlefields of his body. That tired old war. Back to dying by inches, dying by waiting.

He sighed heavily.

The silence in his mind was deafening.

Even if he did beat it, he thought suddenly, it was only a future of empty houses and empty rooms. No one to talk to.

"We think it's controllable. After you recover, we'd like to begin a chemotherapy regime."

"It'd said 'we,' Hersh thought abruptly, remembering the cancer's voice. It'd called us a family.

Had it known about the secondary tumor? Had it considered it a brother? For a moment, Hersh visualized the two of them, sitting there in his body, like kids under the blanket after lights out, giggling and whispering secrets to each other.

Hersh's thoughts moved slowly and clumsily. It was like his mind was wearing thick gloves that made it hard to handle things.

Was this one the promised instrument of revenge? Hersh wondered. A time bomb left behind?

Was it simply a lump of insane cells? A simple malignancy, to be dealt with in the normal way.

Or did this one too have a soul? A voice of its own, waiting to speak?

He wanted to talk about this to the Doctor, but he knew what the Doctor would say.

The Doctor would say it was just a tumor. A part of his body gone wrong; rogue cells multiplying. He'd say that getting rid of it was no more meaningful than clipping your nails. The Doctor would tell him that it was him or it. Kill or be killed.

But what if the Doctor was wrong?

Did he have the right to cut short this brief potential life, simply to extend his own a few more agonizing pain filled months? What if he died anyway? All he'd have to show for it was two innocent voices, untimely stilled.

Empty houses and empty rooms.

Can I murder my children?

"No," he said abruptly.

"Pardon," the Doctor said.

He looked vaguely annoyed at having been interrupted. Hersh realized that the Doctor had been talking, and he hadn't been listening.

"No," he repeated. "No more chemotherapy. No more surgery."

His voice trembled, it was weak and shaky, but something inside him had set firmly.

The Doctor stared at him a few moments. Hersh had no idea what the man was thinking. It occurred to him that the two of them stood at opposite intersections of life and death.

"All right," the Doctor said finally, standing, "in the end, the patient has to decide whether he'll accept treatment or not. I'll give you some time, maybe when you're recovered from surgery, you'll think it over and change your mind."

"I won't. I've made my choice," Hersh whispered back, surprising himself with his firmness.

Hersh watched the man leave. He was so tired. The conversation had exhausted him.

He'd made his choice. But what choice had he made? Hersh wondered, as he drifted off to sleep. Had he chosen life or death? And whose?

Inside his head, it was quiet. There were no voices, not even his own.

* * *

Late at night, Hersh roused to the sound of a figure staggering through the doorway.

It was a nurse, he thought.

Then he saw the gleam of a scalpel, inexpertly clutched.

There Are No Doors in Dark Places – Page 186

The body moved clumsily, as if unused to having to manipulate external limbs.

As it came closer, Hersh could see that there was a strange growth clinging to the nurse's skin, tendrils extended from it, running along the skin and inside the body.

There was a lot of blood.

It must have been terribly desperate, he thought, lying there in the dish, traumatized by the surgery, waiting helpless for the biopsy.

They shouldn't have touched it, he thought. They'd given it one last desperate slim chance, and it had reached for it full of fear and panic, clung and climbed and lashed out.

When it finally spoke, he recognized its voice.

"I'm back."

* * *

Hersh woke.

The room was empty.

"Hello," he said aloud, both fearing and hoping to hear another voice, without or within.

There was none. He was alone in his head again. Whatever voice that had been was stilled.

"Hello," he said.

But it didn't answer.

The End

A Note, plus More Books by the Author

If you've skipped to the end, looking for an apology, well... Sorry? Also, no refunds.

Thank you for taking the time out to read my little book. If you've made it all the way here, then I'm just going to assume you liked it.

I have a lot more stories, several collections actually. Horror with ***Giant Monsters Sing Sad Songs*** and ***What Devours Always Hungers.*** There's comedy and humor with ***Drunk Slutty Elf*** and ***Drunk Slutty Elf and Zombies..*** There are alternate histories – ***Fall of Atlantis, Dawn of Cthulhu*** and **Bear Cavalry**.

Plus novels like ***The Mermaid's Tale*** and ***Axis of Andes***, or nonfiction about ***LEXX, Starlost*** and ***Doctor Who.***

If you liked this, could I suggest you leave a review wherever you got it. Mention it on your blog, or your Facebook. Say nice things. If that's too much, just toss me a couple of stars. Writing is a solitary, lonely pursuit and actually getting some feedback or appreciation is a wonderful thing.

But there's more to it. It's about trying to get out there. There are a lot of people writing a lot of books, and it can get hard to get noticed. Reviews help.

And speaking of writing more....'

Check out my Website, at **denvaldron.com**

HEARTS IN DARKNESS
A Trilogy of Horror Collections

Three Collections of Subversive Horror and Dark Fantasy.

Giant Monsters Sing Sad Songs – The connection between the author of the Necronomicon and a boy in Providence; a girl who meets the last sasquatch, a poet who shares abandoned Tokyo with a Kaiju, and more…

What Devours Also Hungers – The unkillable killers in masks are recruited into the army, vampires and their hunters, clever serial killers, monsters, ghosts and more….

There Are No Doors in Dark Places…..

FUNNY FANTASY
And COMIC SCIENCE FICTION

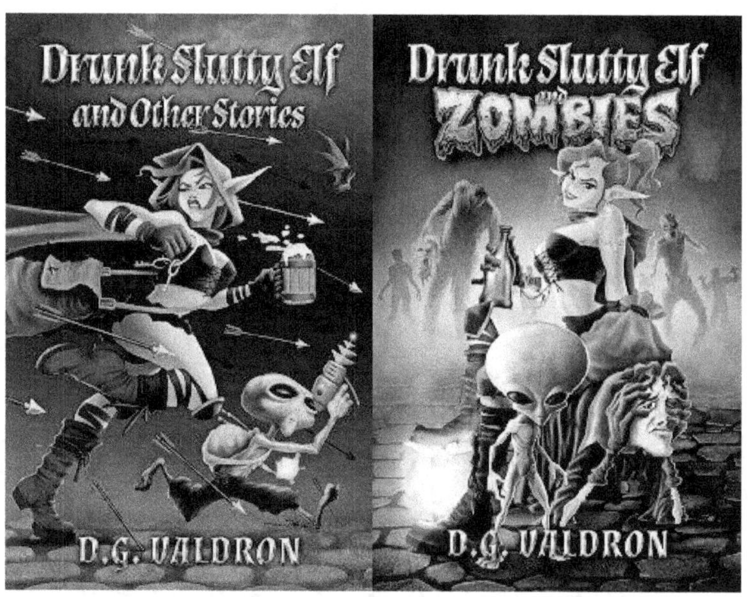

DRUNK SLUTTY ELF AND OTHER STORIES
Plus
DRUNK SLUTTY ELF AND ZOMBIES

Two volumes of savage, satirical, subversive wicked, funny, frantic science fiction and fantasy. Demented ghost hunters, frustrated aliens, horny giants, drunken elves, sneaky ghosts, wayward barbarians and many more.

There Are No Doors in Dark Places – Page 191

A Dark Fantasy of Murder and Redemption

There's a City where all the races come together uneasily, descending into civil war.

There's a Mermaid, murdered cruelly her people distraught and crying out for justice.

There's an Orc, the lowest and the worst, her mission: Solve the murder, before it all comes crashing down.

And there's something else... this world's first serial killer.

Available only as an Audiobook

ALTERNATE REALITIES
A Trilogy or Strange New Worlds
The Other books

The Dawn of Cthulhu - The Secret History of H.P.
Lovecraft's Cthulhu Cult; Lost Continents Found – real and
legendary; The Monsters of Sesame Street, is a light hearted
examination of Muppets as if they were actual animals.

The Fall of Atlantis – Retroverse, An Accidental Cinematic
Universe of 50's Sci Fi movies, Greenland Without the Ice,
Rome Crosses the Altantic, and the Rise and Fall of Atlantis,
an ecological catastrophe.

**The Bear Cavalry, the True (Not!) History of the
Icelandic Bears,** an off the wall, short novel about the
Viking domestication of bears, their evolution into a medieval
cavalry Bonus novelette, The Sharebear Apocalypse.

AXIS OF ANDES
NEW WORLD WAR
A History of WWII in South America

Berlin, 1937, Adolph Hitler and his cabinet meet with a strange delegation from Ecuador. The delegates from the small South American nation beg for help, fearing an impending invasion from their rival, Peru. What happens at that meeting sets in motion a chain of events that sets the entire continent on fire. By the time it's done, millions are dead, nations are in ruins, and the map of Latin America will be changed beyond recognition.

The Pirates Histories of Doctor Who

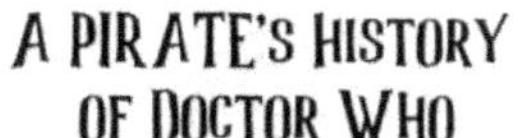

The greatest, Doctor Who fan films ever made, the history of animated Doctor Who, audio Doctor Who, the Stage Plays, explorations of the peculiarities of copyright, the developments of new technologies, the evolution of fan culture, and behind the scenes skullduggery. These books are full of new and entertaining insights and revelations that you'll love.

LEXX Unauthorized, the Series

LEXX Unauthorized about the making of a show about a giant space bug that blows up planets, the cowardly security guard who is its captain, and the undead assassin, runaway love slave, and robot head who form its crew.

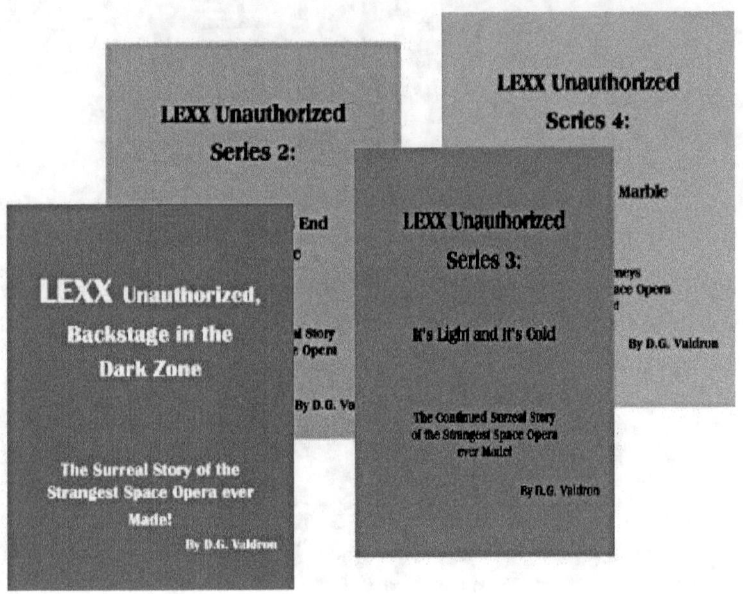

Originally billed as '***Star Trek's Evil Twin***,' the cultiest of cult sci fi, LEXX's forte was black humor, startling visuals, big ideas, and a sensibility that had more to do with surrealists like Jodorowsky or Bunuel than mainstream science fiction. And, as unconventional as it was onscreen, the story of how it came to be is even more bizarre.

There Are No Doors in Dark Places – Page 196

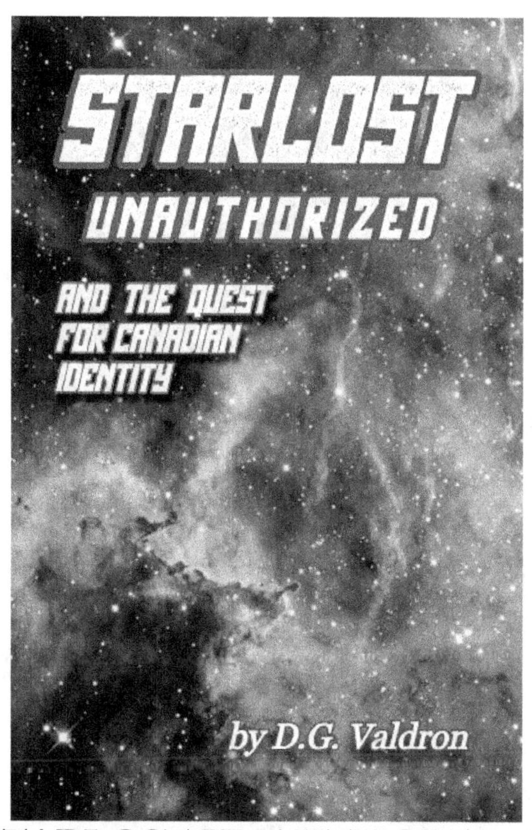

STARLOST UNAUTHORIZED
And the Quest for Canadian Identity

The series that was Harlan Ellison's nemesis. The most controversial series in the history of sci fi television. This exhaustively researched book, based on interviews with some of the stars and writers, brings a fresh new interpretation of of the Starlost, and a re-evaluation of the series and its themes in the context of the 1970s crisis of Canadian nationalism.

TWILIGHT OF ECHELON
Published by
AT BAY PRESS

Based on the work of famed artist Robert Pasternak the book features paintings from Pasternak's Echelon series, accompanied by stories written independently by D.G. Valdron, Lovern Kindzierski, Alex Passey and Blaise Moritz.

There Are No Doors in Dark Places – Page 198